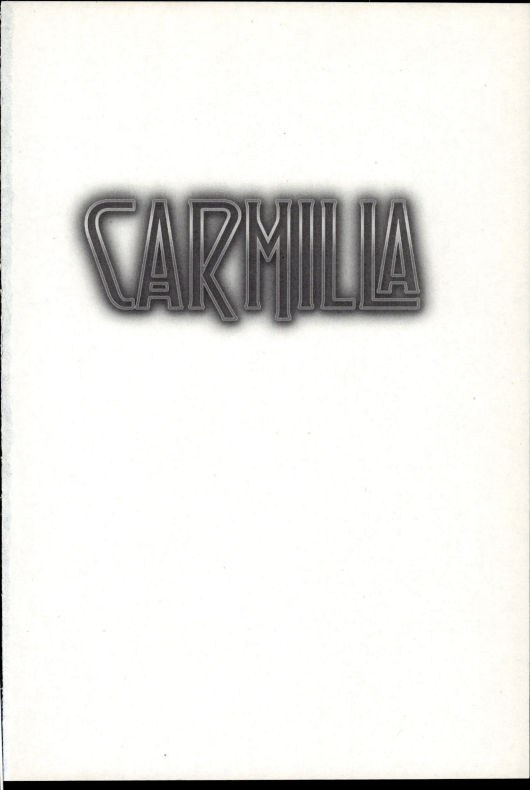

CARMILLA

ADAPTED BY KIM TURRISI

KCP Loft is an imprint of Kids Can Press

Kids Can Press gratefully acknowledges the financial support of the Government of Ontario, through Ontario Creates.

Published in Canada and the U.S. by Kids Can Press Ltd.
25 Dockside Drive, Toronto, ON M5A 0B5

Kids Can Press is a Corus Entertainment Inc. company

www.kidscanpress.com

The text is set in Minion Pro and Bebas.

Edited by Kate Egan
Designed by Emma Dolan
Cover photography by Ashlea Wessel / Courtesy of Shaftesbury

Printed and bound in Altona, Manitoba, Canada, in 12/2018 by Friesens Corp.

CM 19 0 9 8 7 6 5 4 3 2 1

Library and Archives Canada Cataloguing in Publication

Turrisi, Kim, author
     Carmilla / adapted by Kim Turrisi.

ISBN 978-1-5253-0130-8 (hardcover)

     I. Title.

PZ7.1.T87Ca 2019   j813'.6   C2018-902018-0

· ONE ·

The day I've been counting down to has finally arrived. I'm moving into my college dorm. Being an only child has its advantages, trust me, but the invisible shield that my overprotective father has had around me is getting old. I'll be free of the chains once I land in my dorm. Silas University, I'm all yours.

The drive has been excruciating with my father's nonstop chatter. I barely notice the fog roll in over campus as we arrive. Silas is an institution in Styria, Austria. Built in the 1800s, it has castle-like architecture that's haunting yet regal. Ornate archways decorate all of the building entrances. Magical. Weathered stone buildings housing students and classrooms surround a green quad crisscrossed with cobblestone paths. It's perfect.

The renowned journalism program and small class sizes

originally attracted me to Silas, but now I'm all about the campus lore. I mean, for starters, there's supposedly some weird glow from the Aquatic Center after dark. I've always loved inexplicable phenomena. Can't wait to check that out.

"Laura, I know there's a lot to do here but your number-one concern is school and keeping your grades up," my dad says. Here we go again. My eyes fight hard not to roll, but they fail miserably. "If you don't get the grades, we'll pull you out." He adjusts his voice to sound as tough as nails. "I want you to be able to support yourself, not need another person to survive. To do that, you need a college education with grades that help you rise to the top."

Dig deep, Laura Hollis, I coach myself, willing the butterflies out of my stomach. He's got me on edge. Like being an incoming freshman in a school where I don't know one person isn't enough. "Dad, I get it. Trust me, it's all I've heard since I got accepted," I say. I feel guilty for snapping at him, but it's not the time to pound his lesson into my head.

"Laura, this is what fathers do," he explains.

"Drive their daughters crazy?" I ask, half kidding. At least he laughs.

A slight mist starts to fall as we haul my stuff from the parking lot. The sidewalks are lined in a damp moss. I glance up and see ominous dark clouds hanging over the campus. When I open the double wooden doors of the dorm, a chill washes over me. I adjust the collar of my jacket to warm my neck and continue down the hall, scanning the room numbers. Dim lighting gives an amber glow to the walls, and I can hear the faint sounds of other students getting their rooms set up behind closed doors.

"They could use some heat in here," Dad remarks. I'm shivering, but I'm not sure it's from the cold.

We walk down the hall past rooms 305 ... 306 ... The doors are decorated with a variety of pictures, posters and streamers. "Room 307, that's me!" I announce. A sign on the door says, WELCOME, LAURA! XO, BETTY. She's my new roomie. I like her already!

The door's ajar, so I kick it open with my foot. It's a pretty typical dorm room, with two beds, two desks and a teeny kitchen. But we have a big window! Bonus. I peek out and see that we overlook the quad. Nice. The goth architecture combined with the gold sheer curtains hanging from iron rods is giving off a very cool vibe.

It's pretty much the polar opposite of my room at home. My roommate has a flair for decorating. There are countless Zen touches all over. Lavender candles, even a Buddha statue. Back home, Dad is a stickler for less is more. He doesn't like anything chipping the paint, so my room is as sterile as a hospital and just about as inviting. I take a deep breath. I'm so ready for all of this. The adventure, the freedom, all of the new experiences. It's really happening!

Betty isn't here, but her side of the room is cluttered with piles of clothes against the wall and a bed that's semi-made —

really more like a bunched-up comforter on top of a wadded-up sheet on a thin mattress. I throw my suitcases on my bed and look for the closet.

"Do you want to grab some dinner before you unpack?" Dad asks.

"I'm not really hungry. I just want to get settled, you know?" I say. If I'm being honest, I just want to be alone to absorb all of this goodness. I worked my ass off to get here, and I'm ready to start.

"All right, kiddo, I'm going to head home and leave you to it." He's intense but I know he means well. I give him a big hug, and Dad's arms around me feel safe. Warm. A tiny pang of fear sneaks in. I'm really on my own. I step back hesitantly and steel myself for the actual moment he leaves.

"Studies first. Eye on the prize. The TV internship." The coveted internship that I've had my sights set on for the last two years. Working in the research department behind the scenes of a morning show. Basically my dream job. *Stick to the plan*, I scream in my head. Slay my first two years at Silas and I have a shot. My dad believes it, just like I do, and that's what I'm thinking as he walks away. I put some music on to help with the monotony of unpacking. Gwen Stefani is always good for a pick-me-up. I'd folded all my T-shirts and color coordinated them so I could just drop them into the drawers in my dresser. I find a plastic bin in a suitcase, open it and start to laugh. Dad loaded me up with all my favorites: endless cookies, Pop-Tarts, soda and chips. He thought of everything.

I rip open the Oreos and munch on a few while I put away my jeans and jackets. Sounds from outside interrupt me, but when I look out the window, all I see is darkness. Is anyone even here? It's eerily silent, inside and out.

But when I whirl around, I see a girl in a pink skirt wearing neon Chuck Taylors and a smile for days. She's got a pizza box in one hand and a six-pack of beer in the other. Where did she come from? "I didn't even hear the door," I say, a little weirded out. "Um … hey."

"You must be Laura. I'm Betty. Gwen Stefani, I love her!" She sets her food down and rushes to hug me. Her energy is electric. "Cookies! My kind of girl. I thought we should celebrate. Hope you like pizza. And beer."

"Pizza is pretty much my favorite thing in the world. A close second to cookies," I admit. I'm indifferent to the beer. She opens two bottles, expertly, and hands one to me. We clink.

"To a killer year," Betty cheers. She flips open the pizza box in the middle of her bed where we both sit cross-legged. I'm elated when I see sausage and cheese on the pizza. No vegans here. Betty folds her slice and talks while she chews. "This week is frosh week. That means parties on top of parties. The best."

"How do you know all of this already?" How long has she even been here? I wonder.

"Family friend who's a senior is on the student council. She's been on campus for almost two weeks. I drove up with her, so I know what's going on."

Impressive. Nonstop parties, though? I shudder at the thought. My course load is pretty intense. I can't imagine a whole week of parties. I came here for the killer journalism program, not a hangover. But I don't want to get off on the wrong foot on the first day.

"Wait till you meet the Zetas. So many cute guys to choose from," Betty reports exuberantly.

Wonder if now is the right time to tell her that those Zetas do not matter to me regardless of their hot factor or any other attraction she might have? So not my type. I'm still not great at this, even though it's who I am. I just don't want any push-back or bullshit about it. Certainly not on day one. On the other hand … what the hell? May as well put it out there. "Actually, I'm gay, so the Zetas are all yours," I say.

Betty doesn't miss a beat. "Awesome. Wait till you meet Danny. She's one of the teaching assistants. Third year. She's gorgeous and so nice. She even makes me question things. I'll be your wing girl."

"You're on," I say, smiling. I'm already glad this girl's my roomie.

I take my second piece of pizza and she opens another beer. "You ready?"

I pretend I'm considering it. "I still have half left. I'm good."

"You better get in practice," Betty jokes.

I go with the flow and half nod. No need to make waves or stand out, but beer is definitely not on my top-ten list. A final swig of the backwash at the bottom makes me gag. I make a mental note to find a different beverage.

The open door to our room slams shut. I get up to close the window but it isn't open. Where's that breeze coming from? Is there always a draft here? I zip up my sweatshirt, then sit on my bed next to Betty.

We yap until well past midnight, filling in the blanks of roommates 101. Betty is an only child like me. She'd pick a cat, whereas I'm more of a dog person. I'm allergic to cats — at least that's what my dad told me when I asked for a kitten for Christmas when I was six. Betty swears she'd walk over cut glass for a brownie. I feel her. It's like we've been friends forever! We exchanged a couple of emails before we got here, but I had no idea she would be the perfect match for me. Crawling into bed, I almost fall asleep before my head hits the pillow. The tapping that sounds like it's coming from inside the walls creeps me out, but exhaustion takes over. It's my first night at college and I won't think about what could go wrong.

· TWO ·

It's been a whirlwind week — as promised — for the freshmen. My roommate rocks, but she's just what Dad was afraid of — a total party machine. While I burn the midnight oil with my books, she hits any and every party on campus. Didn't miss a single one this week, sometimes two in one night. Confession: she's having way more fun than me. We've been sharing cooking duties and have dinner together before going our separate ways. She makes a killer mac and cheese, but I'm more of a throw-everything-in-one-bowl kinda cook.

Betty made sure to schedule late-morning classes so she can sleep in. My classes start at eight, before any thinking person is out of bed. My day is practically over when hers is just starting.

Clad in my go-to outfit, plaid pajama bottoms and a T-shirt, I start setting up my computer for my first journalism project, a vlog about this storied school. Yep, I'm delving into the mysteries of Silas University, because the folklore surrounding this place is truly legendary. It's shrouded in mystery after mystery: there's even a question about whether there are real eyeballs in the eyeball soup. Okay, the campus myth that unlucky scholars who linger too long in the library might find themselves digitized, trapped for eternity in the online catalog, has me on red-hot alert. No one knows how it happens, only that it does. But I'll get to the bottom of these mysteries with my journalistic skill.

My epic project will land me the A my father expects. I mean, keeping a vlog isn't hard-hitting journalism on its own, but I'll use it to keep all my facts straight for the paper I'm going to write. That's the road to the best grade in class.

"All right, let's do this!" I yell at the computer screen, trying to fire myself up for the beginning of the weekend. The commotion at our door shuts me up when Betty swirls in like a hurricane. Did she really wear a sequined skirt and ripped tank top to class? I wouldn't mind tapping into some of her confidence, but maybe Silas is my chance to do just that.

"How did you do on the government test?" I ask.

She shrugs. "A sixty-two. So, not bad?"

"If I got a sixty-two on anything, my father's brain would explode, then he would order me to move home." And, okay, I wouldn't like it, either. The one time I got a C in high school geometry, I cried for a week.

"You're better than that," I tell Betty, but she's already moved on. Tossing her backpack off to the side of the bed, she roots through the mini fridge and takes a beer from her shelf. She raises the bottle to me and changes her clothes between swigs of brew.

"Shouldn't you be studying?" I ask sheepishly. Her laugh says not so much.

"It's Friday night. There's a raging party in the quad. Everyone will be there. You need to come," she lectures while rifling through the closet for the perfect outfit. Articles of clothing fly through the air, landing everywhere.

"I don't know …"

Betty grabs my hands and twirls me around. "I do. You're eighteen years old. There's plenty of time to study. You've been at it all week. Come on, we need to get you into something besides those pajamas and get you out of this cave. You're withering away. Plus, Danny will be there," she adds, all singsongy.

Not gonna lie. *That* gets my attention. I mean, she's my teaching assistant in women's studies and all, but not my teacher. Big difference. Turns out that's just the push I need to join the Silas student body tonight.

When I met Danny last week I was so tongue-tied that she must think I'm an idiot. At the very best, she probably realizes my game is that I have none. Thank God Betty was there to run interference. (By that I mean speak in complete sentences without swooning.) Danny's flaming red hair cascaded down her shoulders and her smile was as bright as the sun. Just remembering gives me goose bumps.

I take Betty's fashion advice and lose the jammies in favor of a skirt and white tank top. I run my fingers through my hair and add some pinkish lip gloss.

Betty even compliments me. "You're hot," she says.

I check myself out in the mirror. I clean up pretty well. Now to get Danny to notice. I'm so rusty — I haven't had a girlfriend since junior year, when Aisha Carson crushed me, leaving me to wallow with a broken heart for the rest of high school. Pretty crappy timing. I ended up going to prom with some rando setup. My dating skills need some work. Okay, a lot of work.

Betty and I walk arm in arm to the party. The lights lining the walkway flicker as we stroll through campus. Or are my eyes playing tricks on me? Betty doesn't seem to notice. My eyes dart back and forth when the low howl of the wind stirs up the fall leaves. I hear crunchy footsteps behind us, but when I glance over my shoulder there's no one there.

When we step into the party, multicolored strobe lights nearly blind me. My sandals stick to the floor, and I can't get away because hundreds of students surround me, gyrating while they juggle drinks.

A guy hands a bottle of vodka to Betty. "Ten-second pull, let's go!" I watch as she puts the bottle in her mouth and drinks for a full ten seconds. She doesn't even choke.

"I love this game!" she screams over the music. "Your turn. Start small. Five seconds." She hands me the bottle.

A few kids surround me. "Drink. Drink. Drink," they chant. Reluctantly I take the vodka. I want to hold my nose before I sip it, but I also want to be one of them and fit in. Betty starts the stopwatch on her phone. "Go!"

I suck up my fear and bring the bottle to my lips. I'm pretty sure half of it is running down my chin but I manage to continue until Betty calls time. I thrust it back into Betty's hands and almost cough up a lung. Man, this stuff burns.

"Fun, right?" Betty says.

"Yeah." I just hope I don't puke.

Betty points to a group in the far corner wearing green glow sticks around their necks and carrying neon drinks. "Steer clear of them. The Alchemy Club. They do weird experiments that you don't want to be caught in the middle of. Trust me."

Oh, I will, I think. I've never been anyplace else with such a mix of creepy and crazy. Now I'm caught in a sea of wasted people, and I need to find a corner to catch my breath. I turn to ask Betty a question, but she's vanished. Panic starts to set in, when a tap on my shoulder startles me. I turn to see Danny, and a five-alarm fire blazes in me. *Stay cool*, I plead with myself. *Do not babble. Please.*

"Betty's up on the bar — she's doing Jäger Bombs. She's owning them." Danny points across the room. "She's really something."

"Yeah," I manage.

"It's nice to see you out," she says, grinning.

I shift closer to her. "It's nice to be seen" just falls out of my stupid mouth. "I mean, Betty talked me into getting out of my pajamas. You know, to come here. I guess pajamas are frowned on at parties." I just babble. And. Babble.

Danny doesn't seem to notice. "You're cute."

I feel the red spreading across my cheeks.

"Dance?" she asks.

Grateful for the liquid courage I was cursing a few moments ago, I answer with a smile. The touch of her hand on mine as she guides me through the maze of people to the dance floor makes my crush on her grow exponentially. She's just so everything.

And we have the whole year ahead of us.

·

My tongue seems to be wearing a wool sweater this morning. This is exactly why I don't go to parties. I let Betty talk me into all of those vodka pulls and Jäger Bombs, and now I'm paying the price. I look over at the lump beneath her covers. Betty. She ruled the party last night. She is officially the queen of vodka pulls at Silas University, or so said all the screaming students who were cheering her on. With each chug from her perch on the bar, the noise from the crowd was deafening.

The light on my computer is flashing. Crap, I left the camera on. I roll up out of bed and down an entire bottle of water while I scour the room for something for my pounding headache. I spot the bottle I need in a sea of cosmetics on my dresser. Fighting with the childproof top, I yank it off and pop two. I yell to Betty, "How's the Jäger-Bombinatrix this morning?"

No response. Not even a stretch. I know she's sleeping, but no one is going to need this more than she does. So I yank the covers back.

Nothing but pillows.

And then, before I turn away, a piece of folded paper flutters to the floor, stuck together with some unrecognizable fluid. I pry it open. "Dear Student, your roommate no longer attends Silas University …"

I knew it. I knew that party was a mistake. I should have insisted we stay home, but no, I succumbed to the pressure to fit in, to be a normal college freshman who chugs beer and hammers shooters on a Friday night instead of studying. And now Betty is kicked out of school? I text her on my flip phone. Yeah, my dad thought I'd sext selfies to strangers on an iPhone, so this was my only option. He gives new meaning to the words "better safe than sorry."

My first text goes unanswered. Another also goes into oblivion.

My mind starts racing a mile a minute. I mean, I go from zero to one-eighty. Whatever her future is at Silas, where is she now? What if she's lying on the side of the road?

What kind of roommate am I? Did I lose her or did she lose me? *Calm down, Laura,* I tell myself. *We're at college — maybe she hooked up with someone. That has to be it.* My inner dialogue seems to be working. My heart rate is slowing down.

I scan my computer, checking her social media. Nothing since the pic of us playing flip cup with Danny and a couple of knucklehead Zetas. Betty's a poster. I mean, she posts her every move. Her breakfast. Her outfits. Everything. So why the silence?

My heart picks up its pace again.

What can I do but text? *Hey, not to be a freak but are you alive? Hookup?*

I add a laughing emoji to lighten it up and force myself to lie back down. That lasts about forty-five seconds before I pop up to check my phone. Nothing. Maybe I need some cookies.

I rip open a box of vanilla wafers. She's definitely missing. I pause. Do I want to be the overreactive friend who panics? Maybe she's fine.

What if she's not?

I comb the college directory to figure out who to call. I pound in a number in the housing office, hoping someone will answer at this ungodly hour on Saturday morning. I shake the vodka cobwebs out.

"Yes! A person!" I scream when I hear a voice on the other end of the phone. "I want to report a missing person." I don't even wait for a response. "My roommate disappeared last night and all I found was a sticky note, and there is no way in hell or Hogwarts that she would bolt in the middle of the night and leave me with a cryptic scrap of paper."

Plus, she was too drunk to do anything other than pass out. I keep that fact to myself. She was just drunk. Now she's gone. Simple.

"No." I interrupt the lame-sauce BS they're feeding me. "No one leaves a multiple-choice note," I insist. That's the weirdest part of all.

I listen, bobbing my head, then I cut the guy off. "Sir, this is what was left behind. I will read it to you word for word so that you can comprehend the situation.

"Dear Student,

Your roommate no longer attends Silas University. He or she has (a) lost his or her scholarship and has decided to go home; (b) elected to attend another school due to your extreme incompatibility [please, never]; (c) experienced a psychological event that left him or her unfit for student life or (d) cited personal reasons, and really, why does anybody do anything? Exit procedures have commenced. No action on your part is needed."

Obviously, this is a load of crap. It doesn't make the least bit of sense. But I listen. Listen some more. Until I can't stand another word. I take a deep breath and try to be reasonable. "Sir, I don't think you're getting the drift of this. I do not need a new roommate. My old roommate is perfect. It's just that she vanished last night. Disappeared. Something is terribly wrong. I can feel it."

He explains that some kids just flip out and not to worry, they'll get me another roommate shortly. He mentions that I'm overreacting. He's clearly not getting it.

At the end of my rope, I holler, "Obviously you're refusing to help me! I demand to talk to a supervisor!"

"You can't hang up on me!" I scream to no one. I'm ready to throw the phone across the room, except where would I even replace a flip phone? I know I can be a tad high-strung but my gut is telling me that we are at DEFCON 1.

Betty, where are you? I wait a few minutes, then my texts get a bit more frantic. *You need to text me before I call the police. I need to know that you're ok. NOW.*

Crickets.

So I'm on my own in my quest to find my missing roommate. This calls for all the junk food, starting with more of these vanilla wafers and maybe some chips. I find a number for campus security, but my phone rings before I get lost in the automated abyss.

"Yes, I am the one with the missing roommate. Thank you so much for calling." Finally, someone who cares. I listen to the babbling and I have to cut her off right away. Why do these people not get it? "No, I do not need a new roommate! I need to find my old one. She's missing!" I shout. Once again, I'm silenced by a dial tone.

My laptop is the only sign of life in this room. "Fine. If no one wants to help, I will find her myself," I say. "I'm not backing down." Yes, now I'm having a conversation with a computer.

I don't know how, but I will. I close my eyes, willing my head to stop pounding.

This is basically my father's worst nightmare about college come to life. Hangovers, debauchery, kidnapping. Maybe it's all a bad dream. I get back into bed, hoping to start all over by going to sleep.

I toss, I turn, I get caught in the covers like a fish in a net. I try counting sheep, meditating. Nothing works, so I throw the sheet off and get up.

I make a cup of coffee and drag my fingers through my hair. How the hell am I gonna pull this off? I have to find a way. People don't just disappear in the middle of the night. Do they?

A noise outside of my door startles me ... but not as much as when it opens. Standing smack in the middle of the doorway is a raven-haired girl wearing black leather pants and an attitude for days, looking like she's fresh off a Harley. She unnerves me. "Who are you?"

"Carmilla, your new roommate, sweetheart," she answers. Why does she seem so ... superior? She's the new one here.

"Um, no," I say hesitantly, "there's been a mistake. This isn't happening, I have a roommate."

She blatantly ignores me, reaching into the fridge and helping herself to one of *my* sodas. "Don't you catch on fast."

I double back. "No. I mean I have a preexisting roommate, her name is B-Betty," I stammer.

Carmilla surveys the room. "Really? Where is she?"

"She's missing," I snap. This girl is really getting on my nerves.

She strides around the room like she owns the place. Never taking her dark eyes off me, she waves a piece of paper in my direction. "Well, I live here now, per my letter from the dean of students. And no one dares to question her." She's sarcastic but serious. She's ballsy, I'll give her that.

Carmilla tosses her backpack on the bed, then starts ransacking Betty's stuff. Tossing aside her jeans, picking through her pile of clean laundry. When she picks up Betty's shirt, holding it up to herself, I flip. "Hey, that's not yours." Jesus Christ, what is wrong with her?

Her lips turn up and she cocks her head. "It's on the bed that's now mine. Possession is nine-tenths of the law, cutie."

I don't like the way she says that, so I snatch the shirt away from her.

Carmilla shrugs. "Until you cough up Betty, I'm your new roommate and this is my side of the room." She draws an invisible line between our beds with her index finger. She grabs the cookies from my desk and plops down on Betty's bed, scrolling through her phone and munching away.

"I'll find Betty so fast that there will be scorch marks on those leather pants of yours."

The grin on her face rattles me.

And that's before she blows me a kiss.

• THREE •

After another night of insomnia, I stare at my stack of textbooks. I'm certain I look like a wreck. Rat's nest for hair, ice cream stains on my T-shirt. I'm surrounded by coffee, cookies and a box of my favorite chocolate-crunch cereal, attempting to start the outline for the big paper that counts as half of my grade. I don't have one single word written, and I never procrastinate. College is hard. And different. At least this one is.

After half an hour, I have to admit I just can't concentrate. I'll work on my journalism project instead. It's turning into more of a detailed video account of the manhunt for my lost roommate. Hey, that's a strange phenomenon at Silas University, right? Every time I try to talk about anything, it turns into my quest to locate Betty.

Carmilla is nowhere to be found, which is fine by me. The

less I have to interact with her, the better. I wish she was the one who was lost.

I turn the camera on and begin my vlog entry, keeping my voice low just in case. "Betty is still missing and she has been replaced with the roommate from hell. Look at this footage." I click a link to what the camera caught while I was in class this week. "She steals my chocolate, she wears Betty's clothes, she's never up before four o'clock and there's a nonstop stream of girls in our room. Check this out — this is a girl from my anthropology class with Carmilla on my bed."

Danny should be there with *me*.

"Carmilla is the worst."

I dunk a Pop-Tart in my coffee. "Well, guess what," I continue. "I told the girl of the week that Carmilla has a longtime girl-friend. She went crazy. *Bam*, revenge is mine. Now, I'm gonna use her soy milk on my cereal." Maybe no one is following my video blog, but I sure feel better.

I reach into the fridge for her box of nondairy blech. MINE is scrawled in black Sharpie across the front, like she has to protect it. She has one thing in the fridge and lays claim to it while eating all of my food as she pleases.

I pop open the box and pour the soy milk all over my cereal. And I'm not gonna lie — I feel smug and victorious until I look down. The shrieking sound I'm sure the entire campus just heard came from the depths of my being.

This isn't soy milk at all.

It's blood. Or something that looks suspiciously like it.

The floor monitor, Perry, rushes into my room trailed by her sidekick, LaFontaine. I mean, these two are never apart. Perry is the dorm's resident worrier, like a mom away from home. She's by the books; rules are her jam. Perry is preppy, straitlaced and so uptight, her rules have rules. LaFontaine is all punked out in an *X-Files* T-shirt and jeans, their short, spiky hair gelled to perfection. Like my high school friend Sam, they're genderqueer.

I am officially freaking out. "Do you see this? It's definitely blood. Isn't it? How could there be blood? This is the most disgusting thing ever. It's *blood*!" I yell, waving my bowl of befouled cereal at them. Carmilla has ruined a perfectly good bowl of chocolate goodness.

LaFontaine and Perry stand close together, exchanging glances. Inspecting the cereal, LaFontaine says, "Well …" Like Carmilla should be innocent until proven guilty or something.

"Come on, you guys, it's blood. For sure. And, it's the only thing that she keeps in the refrigerator. Not a crumb of anything else. She drinks it all the time. Something isn't right."

Suddenly I see a pattern here adding up to who knows what. Carmilla never studies, she's out all night and girls throw themselves at her. She tends to appear out of nowhere. It's spooky.

And, well, the blood.

Perry assesses the situation. "I admit that I find it a bit odd."

LaFontaine nods. "Odd? That's where you're going with this?

No one takes type O in breakfast cereal. She's off. Sounds like there's something terribly wrong with this one."

"Thank you." I almost kiss LaFontaine, I'm so happy to have someone on my side.

Perry dismisses her friend's comment with a tone in her voice that grates on my last nerve. "You are not here in an official capacity, Susan."

"Do not call me Susan," LaFontaine barks. I have to admit that the name LaFontaine fits. I've never known a Susan who could pull off the funky badass that LaFontaine does. I mean, my grandmother's name is Susan. Case closed.

"That has been your name since I've known you, you know, for the last sixteen years," Perry snaps.

"Well, now my name is LaFontaine." They are not giving an inch.

Perry turns to me. "Maybe you should let Carmilla explain. It might be some sort of a protein supplement."

"Right. For extreme hemoglobin deficiency?" quips LaFontaine.

I scoff loudly.

"Not helping." Now Perry's getting pissed.

LaFontaine rolls their eyes. "Sorry, Perry, I know you want to believe the weird here is all Dr. Seuss, but in my world the Alchemy Club tests subjects in the cafeteria and participates in all sorts of bizarre things one hundred percent of the time. Silas is all about the weird, like it or not. As this floor's unofficial truth speaker, I'm gonna tell Laura here to wise up if she wants to survive."

Gulp. "Survive? Carmilla wants me dead?"

"Anything's possible." LaFontaine is not making me feel any safer.

Still acting like everything is roses and unicorns, Perry argues, "A lot can be solved with good communication —"

LaFontaine cuts her off and turns to me and says, "Or a lot of things can be solved with hair and blood samples." Then whips out a syringe. My startled gasp stops any further action.

"I'm a bio major," LaFontaine explains. "It's totally cool. It's what we do."

I can't take it anymore. This place is nuts. The door to my room blows open, but no one's there. It could be just a draft in the hallway, but nothing here is what it seems.

Nothing.

I'm not going to let the bloody cereal distract me from my bigger problem. Why is Carmilla here in the first place? Because Betty is still missing, and it's been days.

"If I'm going to get anywhere, I think I should go to the dean," I tell Perry and LaFontaine. "Surely, she'll get right on this. One of her students has vanished into thin air. It's not normal."

Perry and LaFontaine face each other and shake their heads knowingly. "Yeah, no. That's not such a good idea," they say in unison. This, at least, they agree on.

I'm not understanding. "What good is a dean of students who doesn't help students? Isn't that her job?"

"Well, she's not really known as the warm and fuzzy type. She likes things her way," LaFontaine explains.

Perry softens her tone. "The only thing she would do is assign you another roommate. Carmilla is better than what could be."

"I don't know about that," I argue. "She's awful. She's up all night, drinks blood and is a total slob. Did I mention she drinks blood? There's not one redeeming quality about her. She is no Betty."

"You might get a snorer or hater," LaFontaine insists. "Don't call attention to yourself with the dean. Trust me. Wait it out. I'm sure Betty will come back."

"All the other girls that disappeared did," Perry adds.

All the other girls?

"All what other girls?" I ask, my voice cracking. This is a new level of weird and slightly terrifying, if I'm being honest.

"It's not like they stayed gone. They returned to campus," Perry starts to explain.

Now my head is spinning. "Let me get this straight. More than one girl disappeared from campus and no one said anything? No one did anything?" Or thought to mention it till now?

Perry stammers and backpedals. "It wasn't really that unusual. Girls having fun. Maybe they got a little carried away. You know."

"No, I really don't." A tiny part of me wonders if my dad was right to be worried about me coming here.

"How do you not know this?" LaFontaine asks. "Two girls from our floor disappeared, then showed up a few days later — one in her dorm room, the other in psych lab — with zero memory of anything in between. Like, zilch."

"Why the hell would I just happen to know this?"

LaFontaine gives me the once-over. "Everyone does."

"It was the beginning of frosh week," says Perry. "Week one. There were nonstop parties. You know that. Burning the candle at both ends, twenty-four seven. I'm sure they just had too much to drink."

"Because *that* causes random disappearances?" LaFontaine says.

I stand up, pleading. "You know these girls? I need to talk to them. Now. They might be able to help us find Betty." The answers could be right in front of us! Betty could be back tomorrow!

LaFontaine puts a hand up to stop me. "You need to chill. They're traumatized enough already and they don't need you stirring up those feelings. You're clearly on a mission."

I protest, "But, I need —"

"Dial it down. You can be a little intense."

Then Carmilla arrives, chuckling like she's in on some joke. "Intense is about right," she says. Her tone is like fingernails on a blackboard.

"You must be the new roommate. Welcome to our floor," Perry greets the roomie from hell.

LaFontaine nods kindly in her direction. Carmilla keeps walking toward the fridge. When she bends in, the girls disappear.

I glance in Carmilla's direction. "You won't find your soy, if that's what you're looking for."

She sees the box on my desk. She knows I know. "Lighten up. It was a prank."

"Blood in a milk carton isn't a prank. It's sick and twisted," I tell her.

She bursts out in a belly laugh. "You have no sense of humor. Please. It was food coloring and corn syrup." She totally dismisses me. "Just testing you, Hollis. You failed."

"You're a freak."

"Aw, you're angry?" Her condescending tone causes a visceral reaction. I feel my face scrunch and tense up. Even my eyes shut.

Carmilla torments me. "The bunched-up face you've got going on is hilarious, buttercup."

I hiss, "How hilarious do you think it will be when I get the dean of students involved to kick you out of here?"

That stops her. "Wait a second, you're going to bitch to the dean? I'd pay top dollar for that show. Be my guest." The invisible wall between us is steel. The silence deafening. I welcome the interruption of two girls who show up in our room. Our door is never closed.

The energetic blonde introduces herself. "I'm Sarah Jane and this is Natalie. Perry sent us down to talk to you. She thought you might have some questions we could help with." These have to be the girls who disappeared. Both of them seem ready to talk.

Carmilla just snorts.

"Thanks for coming down," I tell the girls. "I'm Laura. Ignore my sociopath roommate. So … you kinda disappeared at the beginning of the year?"

"Quite the killer interrogation technique you've got going on," Carmilla taunts me.

I will myself to ignore her as Sarah Jane speaks up, explaining. "One minute I was at the swim team's Under the Sea party, downing Fizzy Dagons, the next I was in my dorm room and people were yelling at me. They said I was missing for two days. I don't remember anything. It's like everything is blank."

"How is that possible?" I ask. Sarah Jane simply shrugs.

I turn to Natalie, who's a little skittish and a lot mousy. "What about you, Natalie?"

She twists toward me. "I was at a wine-and-cheese party enjoying a nice rosé, then a day and a half later I was standing in a lecture hall listening to my professor drone on and on about the American Revolution. Like thirty-six hours flew by with nothing in between."

I'm incredulous. You don't just lose days. "You can't remember anything? Nothing out of the ordinary?"

Both girls cock their heads, deep in thought. Natalie says, "Nada about the lost days, but you know, there's a ton of Fireball in the Dagons."

Carmilla can't resist commenting, "Now that's the scoop of the century."

"Fuck off," I snap before turning back to Natalie. I catch Carmilla grinning. I can't believe I let her get to me. Crap.

Natalie thinks for a moment. "You know, there is one thing. I had the same recurring dream a few days before I disappeared. It was really visual."

I encourage her. "Okay, that's something …"

"I was awake in the dark and there was a big black cat prowling under my bed." She takes a step back. Her voice gets increasingly quavery. "Sometimes a shadowy figure in a white dress would appear. Standing over me. I don't remember seeing a face. My throat started to close and I couldn't breathe. It seemed so real."

Carmilla starts whistling the theme to *The X-Files*. Natalie is ruffled now. Her eyeballs start to twitch and so does she. Just when we were getting somewhere, Carmilla had to break the spell.

"What is wrong with you?" I say.

Carmilla shrugs. "I'm out of soy milk — that makes me testy."

Natalie starts fidgeting with her hair and freaks out. "I have to go. Now. I hope that thing doesn't touch your face," she says nervously. She races out the door and down the hall, making a humming sound.

Sarah Jane moves toward the door, too. "Sorry. Nat is kinda PTSD about the dreams. I'm gonna need to go talk her down. That happens a lot since the whole vanishing thing. Humming is supposed to help. It doesn't. See you later."

The whole encounter leaves me shell-shocked. So much to absorb. The dreams are really nightmares that must mean something. But what? Betty didn't mention any dreams.

Carmilla just skulks around the room like a lion stalking prey. She really hangs on to her anger. Munching on some of my cereal right from the box, she says, "Seriously, if someone's going around kidnapping girls, I can see why they threw those two back."

"Oh my God, you are the devil. If you don't stop acting like this, I'm going to punch you in the throat."

Carmilla sticks out her lip, "Oh, cupcake. So violent."

"That was a real person who had something traumatic happen to her. As a freshman, I see it as pretty much my worst nightmare. I can relate. If I disappeared, would anyone care that I was gone? Or even notice?" I'd really like to slap her but my better judgment takes over. I'm not an aggressive person. Yet.

Carmilla keeps shoveling cereal from the box into her mouth.

"Are you so damaged that you're incapable of caring about anything or anyone?" I fire off.

She gets inches away from my face, so close that I feel her

warm breath as she spews bits of cereal at me. "Do you really think you're doing anything to help that girl? Or Betty? Come on, Hollis, be honest here. Do you know anything that you didn't know before she vanished?"

I don't have a comeback for that. She is 100 percent correct.

"That's what I thought." She circles me like she's about to devour me. "You're a child. You understand nothing. Not about life, not about this place. Nothing. And certainly not about what it takes to survive in a world like Silas." Carmilla grabs my shoulder, sending an electric shock through me. "Word of advice. The sooner you stop playing Lois Lane, the better off you'll be. Trust me." She throws herself on the bed, leaving me speechless. For just a moment.

I take a deep breath. "No. No, I'm not going to stop. The eighteen-year-old who's never been outside the city limits before she got here, who thought that university was gonna be some big adventure full of books to read and parties to dance at, I never thought anything bad could happen. Turns out this new world isn't quite what I thought it was. My university is creepy. Idiots getting hammered. Girls going missing and no one cares. They reappear and no one questions what the hell happened. Maybe that's the way it is but I don't have to accept it. I deserve better. Betty deserves better. Even you deserve better."

She does the slow clap. "Bravo."

In that moment, I know what I need to do. I turn back to my computer and get to work.

Carmilla moves up onto her elbow. From the bed, she asks, "What are you doing?"

"I'm officially changing the core of my journalism project. I'm shifting the focus of my vlog to solicit the students of Silas to help me find Betty. Someone had to have seen something. If the student body pitches in, we can do this together." I almost believe this. I almost believe I can solve this mystery all on my own.

Carmilla purses her lips and blows out. "That's gonna piss the dean off."

"Then she can come talk to me."

Delight spreads across Carmilla's face like a sunrise. "Oh, my money is on that happening. Sooner rather than later. You're asking for trouble."

"I'm asking for answers," I correct her.

"You're crazy."

I stroke a few keys. Voilà. "Hello, students of Silas University, my roommate vanished," I say, firm but calm. "I need your help to find her. She isn't the first to disappear either. No one else will help me, not even the dean of students. But I have faith in the human spirit. If you've seen anything out of the ordinary at a party, message me or leave a comment."

I rewatch it. A little rough but it gets the point across. I post it, then tweet out the link. I'm in business. I'm pretty pleased with myself, feeling borderline cocky. To celebrate, I open up a new bag of chocolate cookies. I'm just about to take a bite when a shrieking alarm sounds.

"What is that?" I panic. A fire drill? A lockdown?

Carmilla is positively giddy, clapping her hands. "Here we go. You've done it now."

Perry races in, full-on execution mode, shouting commands. "Let's go! Town hall meeting! Everybody move now! Remember your training! Five-minute drill! East stairs! Proceed in an orderly fashion!" She gestures for us to go to the right, down the hall. She's signaling like a traffic cop, arms waving. I jump up to follow the others. As I do, I turn around to see Carmilla snatch a cookie. My cookie.

Then mug for the camera as she takes a bite.

· FOUR ·

Rushing across campus to the town hall at dusk, with the alarm piercing my eardrums, I feel the pit in my stomach grow. The winding route to the center of campus takes us through some lush greenery and pooling water that drenches my kicks. Between Carmilla's knowing smile and the hysteria of my floor mates, I'm on the edge of an invisible cliff. Students rush through the imposing double doors of a building that looks like a castle. Or maybe a fortress.

"This was the first building on campus in the 1800s," Carmilla says, seeing me stare at the stained-glass windows. There's a turret at the top, housing a bell. "They used to ring the bell when a meeting was called. That was when it was a much smaller campus. Then they replaced it with the lovely siren, echoing for miles." She sure is full of information all of a sudden.

"What's the town hall for?" I ask. What's the emergency? Do I even want to know?

"It's never good. The dean is usually royally pissed off about something," Carmilla says. "My money is on your silly post."

What? I just posted it. I have nothing to be ashamed of. "It's the truth," I say.

"It criticizes the dean and administration. Not smart, cupcake."

Then we're all packed in the hall like sardines, the entire student body shoulder to shoulder. The commanding presence of our dean freaks me out. I thought she'd be … I don't know. Just not this. I mean, she's like eight feet tall and imposing like a Glamazon. Wearing a tailored suit and a frown, she is all business, but her smoky black eyes are lasers of fury. She could legit be in a comic book.

The dean's tone is measured as she stares out into the audience of terrified students. "Silas has a zero-tolerance policy for posting inflammatory videos of any kind. Spreading rumors about missing students is not okay. If it continues, we will pursue this and the perpetrators will be dealt with."

I swallow hard but keep my eyes straight ahead, not flinching. No one knows what the video is about yet. LaFontaine showed me how to post anonymously. No one even knows it was me (except a few people … like my crazy roommate). Now I just need to keep that secret.

The dean goes on: "I assure you that no one has gone missing from Silas. Rumors are just that."

Right when the dean looks ready to breathe fire, Danny stands tall and speaks. "Excuse me, they aren't rumors, Dean. One of the new members of the Summer Society just went missing from a rush party."

The dean's tone is frozen. "Until that is proven to be fact, it is indeed a rumor."

"Well, the fact is that Elsie went to a party and never came back. And other students have gone missing as well." I know of four so far, I think. Sarah Jane, Natalie, Betty and Elsie.

The dean edges to the end of the stage and burns Danny with a glare. "And your point is?"

"It means women aren't safe on this campus. That's what it means," Danny says. The girl does not back down.

A dull roar emanates from the crowd. Everyone starts shuffling nervously. A guy in back yells out, "Is this true?"

The dean raises her voice to speak above the noise. "Absolutely not. It's nothing more than a manic student taking things a step too far. This university has a zero-tolerance policy for spreading malicious lies. No more videos, or else. Our administration has the utmost commitment to your safety."

"Asshole," Danny grumbles.

I lean toward her to say, "Wait a minute, no one cares about the missing girls. All they care about is a video exposing their inept response?"

"Pretty much."

This place is like nothing I've ever read about, let alone

experienced firsthand. I'm not sure what's more terrifying — the fact that girls are disappearing, or that the dean doesn't want anyone to talk about it. It's like there isn't a single person here who cares about the safety of the women of Silas University. Certainly not campus security who have been no help and now the dean and her administration.

Then things take a surreal turn.

One of the brothers of Zeta Omega Mu charges the stage and takes the microphone. "Yo, bros. It's totally uncool to have the hotties of Silas feeling unsafe going to parties or doing the walk of shame at 4:00 A.M., so we will be designating a brother to protect any girl who's a 7.5 or above."

So happy right now that I'm a lesbian.

Danny tenses. "What a Neanderthal. So faux chivalrous. They're oppressing the entire female student body." I nod in agreement because she's so passionate. And she's even more beautiful when she's fired up.

She yells, "Ladies, we should institute our night marches!"

I have no idea what these are. Marches at night? I'm guessing, but it doesn't matter. I'm joining because I trust Danny.

"Yes!" I yell.

The Summer Society joins her, repeating the chant.

"Night march!"

"Night march!"

"Night march!"

I pump my fist in the air in solidarity. Danny winks at me.

My heart swells.

Then all hell breaks loose. A group of students from the Alchemy Department start to stir. One of them yells, "Night marches will ruin the mycological transition!"

They are weird little creepers. I have no idea what mushroom spores have to do with anything, but they feel strongly about it. Tables start to get upended, the chaos continues.

"Pizza or death!" the idiot Zetas start chanting. Or at least I think that's what they're saying. That's my cue to escape this scene and flee the madness.

Even the dean is dumbfounded when some lunatic throws salted herrings into the crowd. Danny grabs my hand and we hightail it back to my room, dodging chairs, smoke bombs and flying fish.

Later, I lie on the floor, staring at the ceiling in disbelief over what just happened. I realize the dean never actually settled anything about the disappearing girls. All she did was threaten us — and it was all my fault.

Danny comes out of the bathroom, towel-drying her gorgeous, flowing red hair. She smells like a garden, lavender and sunshine. My heart skips a beat.

"Thanks for letting me shower here. They're still working on ours."

In the midst of all the mayhem, Danny's presence gives me butterflies. I can't tell if she's flirting with me or if I'm just having a flirt fest alone in my head. It wouldn't be the first time. She is making my palms sweat. That has to mean something. Right?

"You were so great at the town hall. Standing up to the dean," I gush.

Danny blushes. "It was nothing. It was impossible to just sit in silence while she spewed lies just to save her own ass."

"It was really brave." I can't help myself. "I'm already in trouble, so why not get back to the vlog. Let's introduce you to Silas," I say. Now she knows I'm the one behind the post.

"You're gutsy, Hollis," Danny purrs. Her arm brushes mine, causing a fluttering that I haven't felt in a long time. Not since my first kiss. That thought has my gaze fixed on Danny's lips.

Stop it, Laura. Stick to the plan. Find the missing Silas students.

Danny plants herself next to me in front of the camera on my computer. I slide into the chair next to her, geeking out about being so close to all six feet of her beauty. "Ready?"

"Let's do it?" She grins. Gulp.

I clear my throat and say, "Hello, Silas students. Meet my awesome TA, Danny. She's also a member of the Summer Society, an athletic club here at Silas." Lavender wafts my way as she scoots closer to me. Good thing I'm sitting down.

She adds, "We need your help to find one of my sisters." Her voice cracks and I start to reach for her to comfort her but pull back. That misstep would be awkward. And on camera.

I pick up where she left off. "Elsie disappeared from a party and isn't the first student to vanish. Any details you may have can help. Do you remember seeing her? Her picture is posted in the corner."

"Please help us," Danny adds.

"We're counting on you. Any clue, no matter how insignificant you might think it is, might help us. Signing off for now." I stop filming and post it, linking to all of my social media accounts again.

From the corner of my eye, I catch Danny staring at me. She reaches over and I think she's going to kiss me. I hope she's going to kiss me. Instead, she picks a herring tail out of my hair. Really?

"Thanks."

Her eyes lock on to mine. "Anytime," she coos. I swear, she coos.

"Hey, even though the town hall sucked, I'm glad I ran into you," I say. I feel the heat on my face spreading.

"Same here. I'm thinking we should work together on this. You know, share notes, figure things out while you document the investigation for your class project. I think we make a good team." Her mouth turns up. My stomach does a flip or two.

I see a bat slam against the window, then slide out of sight. The things that occur on a daily basis here can't be happening anywhere else. Silas is a world all its own. A bat? What next?

"Good team," I repeat. My flirt game is truly in need of an overhaul.

She stands up. "Okay, then. I'm going back to my room to get my notes about our missing sister. Should we grab dinner and go over what we've got so far?"

"Sure." I hope I don't sound too eager. It's only dinner.

"It's a date," she says.

The second the door closes, I break into a happy dance. I don't care if it makes me nerdier than I already am. No one can see my keen dance moves but me, and I'm killin' it. The knock on the door startles me — usually people just come in. I fling the door open, hoping Danny forgot something.

No such luck. When I open it, two Zetas barge in. A big dopey-puppy guy who seems familiar and a quiet, intimidating giant. "Hey, little nerd hottie," puppy squeals.

"Um, okay, who are you?" I almost wish Carmilla were here to shut him down.

"We are your designated Zeta Omega Mu safety companions. Escorts. Only dudes. So we're your dudescorts. Awesome, right?" he exclaims.

He's kidding, right? I hope he's kidding.

"Right," I mutter. "Dudescort, do you have an actual name?"

"Kirsch. That's Will," he adds, pointing to the brooding guy in the corner. Kirsch moves closer to me. "I think you have a fish in your hair."

Of course I do. This day keeps getting worse. He flicks it and it flies across the room.

"We were supposed to walk you back from the town hall but

you got away from us. You're zippy." Kirsch bubbles over with enthusiasm.

Zippy.

"Yeah. So it's really nice that you rather large, beefy men want to keep me safe but I'm good. See, I'm snug as a bug in a rug. Totally safe. You can go. Really."

"The girls aren't safe on this campus. We were at the town hall and we're taking action. You need us to protect you."

Do girls really fall for this kind of thing?

"What if you want to go somewhere?" he questions me. He's dripping with sincerity.

"I can handle it."

Will pipes up. "You sure you want to risk it?" He sounds melodramatic and a tad menacing.

"I'm good."

Kirsch keeps shaking his head. "We swore a vow as Zetas. If there's a hottie, we'll be on her." I wonder if he's as dense as he sounds.

"So gallant."

He nods in excitement. "Totally."

I try to usher them toward the door. "I'll tell you what. How about if I promise to call you if I decide to go wandering around in the dark?"

"Really?" Kirsch asks so earnestly that I feel for him.

"Sure," I say. It won't kill me to be nice to him. He's harmless and sweet.

He thinks about it. "Maybe we should stick around. Just in case. Wouldn't want to let a little hottie down."

"Please stop using the word 'hottie.' I have a name — it's Laura."

Kirsch throws his backpack on my bed. "Oh, I know. You're in my lit class. You helped me with that book about that Baobob guy."

"Beowulf?" I say.

"Yeah, him. Of all the hotties — I mean, girls — I asked to protect you specially. I thought we could hang. Since you seem to like that British stuff, I brought these."

He reaches into his backpack and produces a few items, one at a time. "Guinness. Tea. These biscuits, which I'm pretty sure are just cookies but the English kind. I even have a movie about Baobob. Spoiler alert, he has sex with Angelina Jolie."

I don't even know where to start. Then the door bursts open, hitting the wall, and Carmilla storms in, surlier than ever. Will recoils. Kirsch launches into a karate pose ready to pounce.

"What the hell is going on in here?" she growls.

"We're your dudescorts, sexy lady," Kirsch explains.

Will adds, "Here to keep you safe from things that go bump in the night. We'll stick to you like glue, just in case."

Carmilla's head swivels back and forth between Will and Kirsch. "Get the hell out of here before I feed you each other's spleens."

Note to self. Stay out of her path of pissed off. She's fuming.

"Whoa," Kirsch says. "Angry hottie."

Carmilla zooms in on me now. "Why did you let these morons in?"

"They arrived and never left."

"Is this what you were hoping would happen once you plastered your plea on the internet?"

I object. "Um, negative. Not like you've seen my videos anyway."

"Betty's missing. Poor me. My new roommate is mean to me, she eats my cookies," Carmilla whines, mocking me. "Am I close?"

"I don't sound like that. You're so mean," I retort. All right, I'm basically yelling.

Kirsch throws his arms around the two of us. "Come on, babes. You shouldn't fight unless there's a bathtub full of Jell-O or something."

Dear God. How did he get into college? He is a walking stereotype right outta *Animal House*. An old-school classic.

Carmilla shoves him. "Get away from me, you ape."

"He's here to help us." I can't believe I'm defending Kirsch.

"Oh, sorry, I'm so on edge. I just don't appreciate being hauled in front of the dean because of your ridiculous project that's going nowhere, by the way!" she roars.

My heart is pounding. I have to put a stop to all the yelling. None of this is helping me find Betty.

"Truce, Carmilla. I'll put a pin in the Betty investigation

until we can get these fine frat dudescorts out of our hair. How about that?"

She agrees right away. "Deal." I'm immediately suspicious, but she turns all her attention to Kirsch. "My poor, sweet boy," she says, dripping insincere charm. She wraps herself around him like a python. "I have such a bad temper sometimes. Can you ever forgive me?"

Kirsch squirms. "Yeah, sure."

She rubs her nose on his ear. "Hey. That tickles!" he says.

She runs her fingers down his arms. "These arms. And your broad shoulders." The charm is notched up to ten as she runs her lips over his cheek.

"Well, I do work out." Now he's enjoying himself. Not that I blame him — she is really beautiful. Scary, but beautiful.

"I could just eat you alive," she purrs. She's making me blush. She nuzzles his neck. Just as he's getting into it, she chomps down. I mean, digs her teeth right into his neck.

Will pulls her away from his bro dude, stepping between them. "What the hell is wrong with you? He's bleeding." He inches close to Carmilla with his fist cocked like he might just crack her. She not only doesn't flinch, she grins. It's unnerving.

Will backs down, then tugs on Kirsch's sleeve. "We're outta here."

Carmilla sticks her lower lip out. "What's the matter? Not going to stay to protect us vulnerable little girls?"

She's a master. I'll give her that. She has a twisted way of getting there, but I do respect her tenacity.

"You bit me. So not cool." Kirsch acts hurt. I mean, he is literally hurt and bleeding, but his pride took a hit as well. I don't need a dudescort, but I almost feel sorry for him. At least I wasn't on the receiving end of her wrath.

This time.

I'll be sleeping with one eye open from now on.

Carmilla lunges at the guys, sending them scurrying out, fearing for their lives, as she snickers. She's really enjoying herself. As soon as they leave, she flings open the fridge and pops a beer. When she closes the door, I notice the magnets on our fridge spell out VAMPI. I admit I was amused at first when I randomly found half-spelled words on the refrigerator, but now all the creepy is washing over me.

"What?" Carmilla jokes. "It was just a teeny nip."

"You drew blood." I make a mental note to keep at least ten feet away from her at all times.

"You wanted them gone and now they are," she reasons.

"Gone, not dripping blood."

She takes a swig of beer. "So much for the truce."

I know I can't let my guard down, but I wouldn't mind a little peaceful coexistence here. Time for me to step up, if only to save myself.

My computer starts to ping. "Hey, Carmilla. I'm sorry I caused the whole town hall fiasco with the dean so pissed off. I feel bad about that. I really do. But I'm not sorry about posting the videos. And … I'm not going to stop. They're too important."

The pinging continues.

She isn't forgiving, but at least she isn't yelling. "They will come for you. It's only a matter of time before they track the posts to you. The dean is ruthless. There will be no letting up once she pegs you as a troublemaker. Be afraid. Are you really gonna risk the wrath it will bring for your, like, three viewers?"

For such a badass, Carmilla's rattled by the dean. Her voice quavers at the mention of her.

An onslaught of pings drives me to my computer. "Holy hell."

I stare at the notifications and messages flooding the screen. "Yeah, sorry, I don't think a lack of viewers is going to be a problem."

· FIVE ·

I've tried on five shirts already, and there's a trail of clothing across the dorm-room floor. Dates are hard. You don't want to try too hard but you also want to be sure it looks like you've made an effort.

"What's wrong with you?" Carmilla asks.

"Nothing. I have a date."

She sits up in her bed. "Danny?"

How does she know?

"Nothing is a secret in this dorm," Carmilla reminds me.

I nod.

"What are you doing? Going on a search for Betty?" she cracks.

"Ha. Not funny. Dinner."

"So original."

Not like she's had any dates. She's a hookup kinda girl. No strings, so it seems. "Jealous much?" I tease.

She sits up, cocks her head. "Of Danny the TA? Hardly. I just think if you like a girl, you spend a little bit more time planning a date rather than going on some throwaway dinner. Be creative, you know?"

I take a swipe at her. "Well, with the parade of girls coming and going, you must be awfully busy being creative."

"Oh, cupcake. Now who's jealous?"

She's exasperating. I disregard that remark and return to my wardrobe quandary. Black jeans? Too dressy, trying too hard. Just jeans, I decide. I settle on my favorite pair with the winning shirt, number six, a long-sleeved garnet T-shirt.

It's bad enough sharing space with a stranger but even worse when that person is watching your every move. Carmilla glances over the top of her magazine, sizing me up. "Not bad."

I ignore her and leave, obsessing about my outfit all the way to my date.

•

I meet Danny at Tobias Grill, a schnitzel-and-goulash place near campus. She waves me over, and I feel my nerves growing along with my smile as I get closer. How do I greet her? A hug, a *hey*? Suddenly, I'm smack in front of her and before I can even utter *hello*, she's on her feet, pulling me in for the kind of hug that you never want to end.

But it does, because we have to eat. She slides over. "Sit next to me." I notice an order of dumplings already on the table.

"You mentioned that you love dumplings. They have the best in town. I got an order of potato dumplings and one of pork. They'll make you cry," she coos as she feeds me one. I might cry all right, but not because of the dumplings. Though they're amazing, too.

How can I be sitting in here crushing on someone when my roommate is missing?

"Together we'll find Betty. We have to eat." It's like she's reading my mind. Concentrating is going to be a challenge. I catch her eye. Both of them, actually. Deep blue.

The challenge is real.

"These are bites of heaven," I gush.

"It's my one cheat food. I try to stay away from anything carb, but these don't count." Danny throws her head back, giggling.

I nervous-eat dumpling after dumpling.

"Besides the kidnapping thing, how are you liking Silas?" She keeps the conversation going.

Between bites I say, "It's quirky but I'm enjoying being out from under my dad's nose. Experiencing new things. He's really strict. Only-child thing."

"I have two brothers and a sister. Sometimes I wish I was an only child. I've had to share a bathroom my entire life."

"The worst! Sharing a bathroom with Carmilla is pretty bad," I say. "She's a total slob, unlike Betty. The sooner we solve this and get Betty home, the better. I'm tired of cleaning up Carmilla's mess."

By the time we walk across campus again, it feels natural to be hand in hand. "I have all my notes ready to go. We just have to pick them up on the way to your room." We're going to take the next step in the search, though my interest in the project is wavering a little right now. I'm only interested in one person, and she's right here.

"This was a good idea. Strength in numbers," I announce. Anything to make this date last.

She stops walking, places her smooth hand on my face. *Please stop the world right this second and make her put her lips on mine.* Instead, she flashes a smile that makes me blush.

I'm fairly certain the grin plastered across my face doesn't move an inch the entire walk back.

•

Danny and I have command central set up in my dorm room. She brought down a bulletin board, and now we have clippings pinned up everywhere with color-coded Post-its. All these clues are from students who watched the videos of me asking for their help. I asked for information, and they answered. They're reporting what they saw at the parties or around campus — so many messages and comments to sift through.

"Can you believe this?" I ask Danny. I just know the answer has to be here somewhere.

She grabs my hand. "We're getting closer. I think we may have a breakthrough soon. We're geniuses," she brags. Her touch feels like fire in all the good ways.

Carmilla is in bed with her nose in a volume of Kierkegaard. It's as if the only thing she reads is gloom and doom. The darkest philosophers possible. Not a single mention of Buddha from her lips.

She makes a choking sound, like a gagging cat. "Sorry, I suddenly feel nauseated."

Danny turns and gives her a taste of her own medicine. "Oh. I'm sorry. Maybe you should go to campus urgent care."

That makes me snort. Carmilla shoots a death glare at the two of us, then yanks the blanket around her to shut us out. It's okay with me — we have work to do and don't need her bad energy.

"Damn, she's extreme," says Danny.

"You have no idea. But let's not waste time on her. We have a video to make for today's vlog update." So much to do. So many viewers waiting.

Danny moves her chair up to the webcam, adjusting it. I lean over her shoulder and turn it on. My cheek brushes hers, and I'd like to ask her about her soft skin, but I stick to the game plan. Operation Find the Students.

"First of all, thank you all for your messages reporting all the unusual things you've seen on campus. They've been incredibly helpful," I begin.

Danny picks it up from there. "Here's where we are. We know of four girls that have disappeared on campus. All from parties. Two of them have returned. Neither has a memory of what happened. Zippo. Your input is critical."

Without the help of strangers, we may never find the answers. The women of Silas aren't safe right now. Their lives may depend on us.

My turn. "Sarah Jane and Natalie were both having super-creepy dreams before they disappeared. We don't know whether Betty or Elsie were having the same nightmares since they have yet to reappear, but maybe there's a pattern. And no one else got a cryptic note from some apparent authority but me. So if any of you can think of what these four had in common, we're all ears. Signing off."

We turn toward each other, and seriously ... the electricity. I wish I was the girl who grabbed the girl boldly and gave her the best kiss of her life, but I have never been that girl, nor do I show any signs of becoming her ... yet. Here at Silas, I could become a completely different person, but I'm still new enough. For now, I'll just be over here with my heart pounding and stomach jumping all over the place hoping Danny will make a move.

I post the video.

"We're a great team," she says, gently resting her head on

my shoulder. I might die right now. I see Carmilla remove the blanket covering her face, revealing her upper lip rising on one side. What's her problem? Is she snarling?

Our little moment — I think it was a moment? — is interrupted when messages start pinging at breakneck speed. Danny and I are not the only ones who want to solve this mystery. I'm not even the only girl with a missing roommate … though I'm the only one unlucky enough to get Carmilla as a substitute. Trapped like a lab rat with a blood-drinking slob.

For the next several hours, we study the new stream of clues. We test timelines and move around pieces of the puzzle, hoping for some hint that we are on the right path to figuring out what the hell is going on.

No luck. I let my head rest on the desk. "It's highly probable that my brain has melted."

"Nothing that some caffeine and food won't fix," Danny offers.

Oh my God. "I'm the worst hostess ever." I jump up and raid the fridge. I load my arms with soda, peanut butter, caramel corn and brownies before returning to my hungry guest.

Danny takes one look at my haul and says, "Laura, how do you eat that stuff? Do you know how many chemicals are in all of that crap?"

"But they're my favorites and delicious. Plus, in the face of epic failure, this is the comfort food that will get us through," I argue.

"Look, we aren't at *epic* failure yet —"

I interrupt her. "Every time we get close to anything substantial, all of the doors slam closed. I feel like we take one step forward then two back." *How long can we take this?* I wonder.

Danny is all sunshine. "Have faith. We know that each of the girls vanished at a party. That's something. The Under the Sea swim party, the Psychology Department's wine-and-cheese gathering, the North Quad mixer and the Summer Society rush party."

I see where she's going. I think. "All planned by different organizations with unique invite lists."

Danny gets up and paces, ticking off more information that we've gathered. "What about all the party gear? A smoldering caldron for the Fizzy Dagons at the swim party. A three-foot volcanic replica with melted Brie at the wine and cheese. The Summer Society rush party had bioluminescent candy-bugs front and center. Lastly, at the Quad mixer —"

I jump in. "Party Fog."

Danny continues, "All provided by —"

My turn. "The Alchemy Department!"

Can't be them. Can it? They're wannabe scientists, like LaFontaine. Not kidnappers. Nerds are one thing, criminals are another.

"Do you actually think one of them is kidnapping girls?"

Danny hesitates. "It's all we've got. I know it's a long shot but I think it's worth exploring. Don't you?"

"I do if you do," I say. I even giggle. I hear choking from the other side of the room, and it's Carmilla of course, watching our every move. I lift my eyes to see her pouring some of her so-called soy milk on her cocoa puffs. Still looks like blood, if you ask me.

Carmilla throws in her two cents. "Have you seen those Alchemy Club geeks? Most of them couldn't pull off a Band-Aid, never mind some elaborate kidnapping." I swear I hear her scoff at us. But she also has an opinion.

And I hate to admit it but she could be right. I turn to Danny, which gives me a reason to look at her. "Maybe we need to talk to Sarah Jane and Natalie again, see if we can jog their memories."

Carmilla chimes in. "Oh joy. Another visit from little Miss Crazy and Miss Scared of Her Own Shadow. That should be a load of laughs. Can't wait."

Just when she was almost helpful, she turns sarcastic again.

Danny and I sift through more tips while Carmilla buries her head in her doom-and-gloom book, occasionally peeking over the top to sneer at us. She's not as stealthy as she'd like to believe. Every time we giggle, she gags.

Now I'm doing it on purpose. I can dish it out, too. Let's see how she likes to be taunted. May as well make good use of my time while we wait for the girls to show up. I lean in closer to Danny when I see Carmilla look up. This time she starts retching like she may throw up.

I win.

Then a ruckus outside the door gets our attention. Natalie rolls up draped in sequins and owning some batshit-crazy dance moves. Is this even the same girl? Last time we saw her, she was mousy and barely spoke above a whisper. This drastic shift in her personality jars all of us, even Carmilla. Natalie goes right to the video camera and poses in front of it. "This is so dope. Let's do it. Put me on TV." She starts striking dance poses like Drake.

I have to ask, "Are you okay?" I see Carmilla moving her finger in a circle next to her head like "she's nuts." I do not think she's wrong.

Natalie leaps back from the desk, launching into a dance routine to the music that's blasting in her head. "Never better. This is the most fun I've had in my entire life."

"Really? The last time we talked, you were very upset. Almost inconsolable. You know, about the time you went missing? The bad dreams." I hold my breath for her reply.

Natalie throws herself into a chair. "Yeah, they were freaky. I'm not thinking about them anymore. Goodbye to them. Wine coolers?"

Before you know it, she exits as fast as she blew in.

"What just happened?" I say. "That was peculiar even for her." I check the time on my phone — she was here for two minutes. Like, why did she come at all?

Danny and I try to figure it out, but eventually she stands up and stretches. "I have no idea how to explain that. Just wow. I'm beat, so I'm gonna take off. I have an early class."

I hop up. "I'll walk you out."

"It's like five feet to the door," Carmilla says drily.

We both giggle. I boldly throw my arm around Danny. We linger near the door. Just staring at each other. My stomach is tingling.

Carmilla huffs as she moves around us. "I need some air."

More giggling.

When Danny finally leaves, I settle in to make a new video update. Sitting alone in front of the webcam, I launch into what has transpired so far.

"Something is terribly wrong on this campus," I tell my viewers near and far. "Something or someone is turning college students into pod people. Full-scholarship Natalie has flipped into table-dancing, frat-boy-loving Natalie. Talk about a three-sixty. And she's not the only one."

I do my best to sound like a tabloid news reporter, all mysterious and suspenseful. "Sarah Jane. Poor thing. She came to Silas as a premed prodigy. Destined to follow in a long line of family doctors. Until the Under the Sea party transformed her into a beer guzzler. I mean Betty was a partier but ..."

Wait a second. A light bulb goes on. "Or was she?" I say slowly. "Maybe when I met her, they had already morphed her into Party Betty."

I barely realize that the night has passed me by as I go

through countless messages from the student body. Day turns back into night. Twenty-four hours later, still in my pajamas, I've mowed through an entire package of cookies and a bag of gummy bears. Empty, crumpled wrappers littering my space.

Carmilla drags herself out from under her cover fortress and busies herself making hot chocolate. "Morning," she greets me.

"It's 5:00 P.M.," I answer. Her mornings are my evenings. She doesn't do days.

She chuckles. "Wait, did you skip class?"

"I felt sickish."

"You do look like crap," she says. She drops the steaming mug of cocoa in front of me. "Try not to get into trouble before I get back."

It was my cocoa, but that's the nicest thing she's done for me since she swooped in here. "Where are you going?"

"Oh, are you going to miss me?"

Suddenly I'm flustered. "Just trying to be a good roommate," I say. "I've already lost one."

Carmilla softens her stance, half smiles. "Got it. I want to catch a lecture on Goethe. It should be a good one, plus there's going to be an open bar. Don't worry about me. I'll be back before Thursday."

As she leaves, I notice a guy who could double as a were-wolf walking with one of the girls from my floor. He's carrying her books, leering at her. Am I bleary-eyed? Seeing things? Moments later, the dorm is strangely quiet.

In my rush to gather clues, I've never actually googled Betty. As soon as I type in her real name — Elizabeth Anne Spielsdorf — I land on her high school's website. It's enough to get me talking to myself. "Holy crap," I say. "Betty was the valedictorian of her class in high school, student council vice president."

An image search shows an awkward girl clad in plaid with braces. Yeah, this is not my version of Betty. Here she is protesting with a group of nerds. Here she's competing in a debate. I need more caffeine to deal with this. I pop a pod in the coffee maker and watch the liquid magic fill my Tardis mug. I love that thing. Best gift my dad ever gave me.

The sound of clacking heels out in the hallway grows louder and louder. The magnets on my fridge now spell RUN. If only I could. Suddenly, I'm jarred by the sound of the door flinging open, the doorknob hitting the wall.

"Hide, Laura! Quick!" LaFontaine is screaming, running into my room with a distraught Perry in tow.

"It's the dean. She. Is. Coming. Here." LaFontaine is full-blown hysterical. I start to dive under the desk when a booming voice behind me scares me into stillness.

"I'm here to speak with Ms. Karnstein!" I hear the voice bellow. It's like the voice I heard at the town hall, deep and stern and terrifying.

I stand up and lift my head. "I'm sorry, I don't know who that is." Perry and LaFontaine are cowering in the corner, shaking.

The dean clears her throat. "Carmilla. Carmilla Karnstein."

My first thought is, *Thank you, Jesus, that the devil hasn't come for me.*

My second is, *Karma is a bitch, Carmilla. Whatever you did, the dean is here for you.*

"She isn't here, ma'am." I know my voice is quavering but she's very scary. And so tall.

She thunders back, "When she returns, let her know I need to see her immediately. If not sooner." The door closes and I practically sink to the floor.

"The dean never comes to the dorms," Perry says. "Something is amiss."

"Amiss? It's the apocalypse," LaFontaine corrects her.

Then we hear bustling and raised voices outside the door. LaFontaine presses against it, then whispers loudly, "It's her, the dean. And Carmilla."

I sidle up next to them. "What are they saying?"

"I can't make out the actual words. It's like they're screaming through their teeth."

"This is so childish. You two should be ashamed of yourselves," Perry says. Like she doesn't want to spy herself.

LaFontaine ignores her. "Shhhh. I just heard something. The dean just said she didn't go out of her way to get Carmilla accepted to Silas to have her behaving badly. Oh man, she's in trouble."

She got her into Silas? Carmilla is connected to the dean? Why didn't she mention that? Something is up with her.

"Serves her right," I chime in. I know this shouldn't give me as much joy as it does, but it does. She earned every bit of this beatdown. She's been nothing but a thorn in my side since she forced herself in as my roommate.

"Deriving pleasure from someone else's pain isn't becoming, Laura," Perry says, like she's my dad or something.

"After everything she's put me through, it's sooo satisfying."

Meanwhile, LaFontaine still has an ear glued to the back of the door. "Jeez. This is bad. The dean just told her that if she didn't take care of the situation, she would."

"Yes! She so had it coming," I cheer, pumping my fist in the air. The door flings wide open, revealing them both. The dean towers over Carmilla, who stands rigidly, frowning. The conversation is over and she has been released back into our room.

LaFontaine stammers, "Uh, Dean." She sort of bows. "Your Disapprovingness."

Perry attempts to soothe the beast. "So very nice to have you visit our floor. What a lovely surprise and a pleasure," she says.

The dean departs without a syllable, leaving only a whiff of disdain.

We all breathe a sigh of relief — except Carmilla. Humiliated, enveloped in fury, she stomps around the room, kicking chairs and anything else in her path.

Perry can't wait to get out of here. "It's been a blast, but LaFontaine and I have a student crisis or something like that to tend to."

LaFontaine can't resist needling Carmilla. "So can I ask you about the coagulating properties of Karo syrup and food coloring?"

"Let's go," Perry says. "You can ask her later."

LaFontaine hesitates.

"Now, Susan," Perry says.

Leaving, LaFontaine throws two fingers to eyes, then back at Carmilla, letting her know that she's being watched. Not subtle. Not so smart. As the door clicks closed, Carmilla whips a mug at it, sending ceramic shards everywhere. She's really upset. "Do you want to talk about it?" I ask. I'm sincere. I've never seen this side of Carmilla. I've seen her mad, but this is different. She's out of control, so angry that fire is dancing in her eyes.

"No," she growls.

Fine. "Because it isn't badass to have the dean personally rip you a new one?"

"But I had it coming, right?"

That makes me wince. I deserved that. "I didn't mean it like that, Carm," I try.

"Sure you did. You don't think that she raked me over the coals because I ignore your passive-aggressive chore wheel, do you?" She gestures to my expertly color-coded chart that she's ignored from day one. Not one single dish has been washed by her hands.

"No, I don't, but why was she so pissed off at you?"

At first she acts like she isn't going to respond. Eventually, though, she admits that, "I might have said a few things in passing that she wasn't a fan of." Carmilla flops on her bed. I'm not connecting the dots.

"When? At your Goethe seminar?" I ask.

She babbles on, clearly distracted. "This age doesn't understand obligation. It's an undersea anchor weighing you down. No escape. Drowning."

That I get. "Worried that you aren't living up to expectations?" She looks me in the eyes and I stare back. "Listen, I am the only child of a massively overprotective father. And I didn't even have to get all creepy poet about it."

"You're funny," she says. A lightness fills her, and I notice that her gorgeous mahogany-brown eyes mist over, dousing the fire. I hand her a tissue. The moment we are sharing — which is undeniably a moment — is cut short when Danny breezes in. I've got to start locking that damn door.

Danny doesn't know what she's walked in on. "Hi. I'm back from the Alchemy Department with a big win."

That gets my attention. "Please tell me they're the ones responsible for kidnapping all of the girls?" That would shore everything up rather nicely and we could move on. You know, be normal college kids.

"More like they are using dander collected at the parties to seed an immense interconnected fungus throughout the entire campus," she spouts off without taking a breath.

"What are you even talking about?" This sounds like a foreign language that I don't speak.

Danny makes herself comfortable, cross-legged on my bed. I notice Carmilla notice. The hairs on the back of my neck rise.

"It's some crazy communication experiment. But the real headline here is that those creepy little proto-scientists have been photo-tracking every party on campus as part of their documentation," Danny reports, her voice rising with excitement.

"Okay?" I'm not completely following.

She bounds off the bed, snatching my mouse. "Check this out. Access to hundreds of pictures from each of the parties where the girls vanished."

This is it! "Danny, you're brilliant!" I cry. I'm sure my compliment sounds lame but she's amazing. It's the first real break we've had. "Seriously, Danny, without you we would be in the weeds. You really stepped it up."

Carmilla grimaces. She shifts uncomfortably. I almost feel sorry for her. Danny and I are about to become legends: the girls who saved Silas. Carmilla will be just a bystander. That's gotta hurt.

"Sorry, I just remembered I need to be anywhere but here," Carmilla mutters. I knew it was too good to be true. She's back to her salty self.

"Too bad, we were so enjoying your company." Danny is one degree more sarcastic than usual, like she's channeling Carmilla herself. And I can't exactly blame her — it's not like

Carm is welcoming her with open arms. But Carmilla seems almost … vulnerable.

Almost.

The door slams so hard that the walls rattle.

"Knock it off," I tell Danny.

She's baffled. "Why should I?"

"Her day has been epic suckage. Cut her some slack."

"You're too sweet." That's nice, except that I was just thinking that Carmilla was sweet, and now I'm all confused. I can't focus on that right now. We have hundreds of images to sift through for clues.

As we start our assault on the pictures, my eyes start to cross. So many images. So many glasses of Fizzy Dagons being consumed. I don't know how there aren't more pictures of vomit. Minutes turn into hours and I guess I nod off, but Danny's cry wakes me right up.

"I found something!"

I'm listening. "Show me."

Danny points to a girl in a photo. "This is Elsie. At the rush party the night she went missing. Check out the person next to her."

My heart sinks. It's Carmilla. Plain as day.

· SIX ·

I'm gearing myself up for tonight's update, without Danny. I'm solo. I make sure I have the pictures ready to post as I'm prepping for my new video. Tonight is going to blow the roof off. If I'm being honest, I have mixed emotions about all that we've uncovered. All cued up, I turn into a news anchor.

"Hello, Silas student body. It's just me tonight, since Danny had an emergency Summer Society meeting. I know some of you think we're overreacting. Trust me, we're not. Yes, we read all of your comments and messages. It's time to wake up and find the missing students. Check out these incriminating photos and you'll have to admit that things are looking incredibly suspicious. Even her highness, the dean, won't be able to ignore these."

As much as the dean wants to bury this and act like nothing

happened, we aren't going to allow her to do that. We're in this for the long haul. If Carmilla was in trouble with the dean before, things are about to get a whole lot worse.

I post the first damning picture. "The Under the Sea party. Here's Sarah Jane dancing with a half-dressed, totally baked guy. Five feet behind him is Carmilla, my roommate, at a swim team party. She's not on the team."

Then the next. "Now this, the Psychology Department's wine-and-cheese fest for freshmen. What the hell is a third-year philosophy major doing there?" I zoom in on Carmilla lurking in the background, nursing a drink.

I adjust the picture, zooming in on Carmilla's eyes. "Aren't those the most sinister eyes you've ever seen?" To be honest, they aren't always scary. Sometimes they sparkle like diamonds. I refrain from blurting that fact out loud.

I take a dramatic pause like they do on network news before adding the third and final piece of evidence. I mean, photo. I'm channeling my inner Veronica Mars. I mean, Lauranica Mars.

"I give you the final nail in the coffin. Carmilla talking … or is she arguing … with Elsie? You might remember her as the girl I kicked out of my room after I found her in bed with Carmilla." I thrust my fists above my head in victory. "*Bam!* This proves that my lazy roommate is up to her eyeballs in vanishing girls on Silas campus. If she is, history tells me that confronting her is about as effective as using bug spray on

Voldemort." I pause for effect. "So do I start stalking her with my webcam? You bet I do. Stay tuned. Signing off."

I complete my mission of the night by hitting Post. Can't wait to see what this one does to my vlog views — they've been through the roof this week. Then I rearrange the webcam to face Carmilla's side of the room and set it to stay on all of the time. I strategically place a Post-it over the red light. She'll never know. The thing about Carmilla is that she's too dismissive to stay current on all of my videos — she thinks they're stupid. If I'm wrong and she's watching them, then she'll confront me. She isn't one to hold back on anything. Either way, it's a win for me.

Buckling down with a bag of potato chips and grape soda to do some schoolwork, I'm ready to attack this biology worksheet when shouting from the hallway distracts me. Do I hear a body thump against the wall? Before I can look out to see what the hell it is, Danny bursts in. Disheveled, she rushes to my side and takes my hand. "Are you okay? Have they tried to get you?" she asks, all upset.

"What? Who?" She's making no sense.

"The Zetas. They were trying to escort the women's swim team home from the gymnasium and the girls called us for help. They wanted to go it alone. You know, a night march in unity. In the melee, someone shoved someone. Now it's a full-scale turf war for the gym. I didn't think you were out but I had to know you were safe."

I blush. "That's so swee —"

Hammering at the door ruins the moment. Wouldn't you know, I hear Kirsch on the other side. "Hottie Laura, are you all right?"

"Oh, for God's sake," I grumble as I put my hand on the doorknob.

"Don't let him in here, don't open the door," she whispers.

I brush her off. "It's only Kirsch. He's dopey. Totally harmless." Ignoring her warning, I crack open the door.

"I was super worried," he starts to say.

But Danny grabs his ear as he comes through the door. "Ow!" he says.

"Danny, you're hurting him." She's latched on like a gator.

He stumbles when she lets go, his ear bloodred. "Why are the hotties in this room always so violent?"

"Because you're an idiot," Danny snaps.

"Not cool, Summer Psycho."

"I can't believe you let him in. He's probably trying to take over our dorm for the Zetas."

So it's an actual turf war? I have no idea what's going on here.

"Am not!" he screams. "We are here to protect —"

"The only thing we need is for you and your frat buddies to get the fuck away from us." Not sure who this Danny is, or what set her off, but we need to rein it in here. I thought we were all on the same team.

I get between them, risking life and limb. "Why don't we take a breath? Chill out."

Kirsch reaches over my shoulder and points at Danny. "If you weren't so hot and, you know, a girl, I'd kick your ass."

Danny shoves him and shows her fists. I can't believe this is happening. "Bring it, frat douche."

Kirsch lunges at her. "I'm not afraid of a girl!"

She punches his shoulder. "This girl isn't afraid of you either."

I swear this is like being on a playground with six-year-olds.

The two continue to go at it while the sound of cherry bombs, or something like them, explodes outside of our window. The metaphor isn't lost on me.

Kirsch tries to take Danny down in a wrestling move that leaves him in a headlock. She bends his neck and tightens her grip.

"You're so mean," he groans.

"Stop it, stop it, stop it!" I yell. "I know you both have the same intention to keep the campus safe, but has it occurred to you that while you're wasting time behaving like children, no one is protecting anyone at all?"

Danny lets go of his neck. "They started it."

"Really, you're going with that?"

Kirsch gets back in her face. "We totally did not."

"Maybe you two spare me the smackdown in my dorm room and try to talk some sense into the disgruntled students lighting cherry bombs and setting random stuff on fire."

"I knew you were smart from that first day in English lit." Kirsch sings my praises before turning his attention to Danny. "She's the smartest."

"Indeed she is."

"And a total hottie. Double jeopardy." He can never just leave well enough alone.

That's enough for Danny. She pivots to Kirsch. "Since you're taking your newfound job as chief protector so seriously, I think it's time for you to get back to it. Fight the good fight."

Her patronizing tone goes over his head. His mood turns serious. "You're right. I'm on it." He slips out the door, leaving Danny and me alone.

"So I should probably go?" she asks.

I want to scream, *No, stay with me. Put your arms around me. Kiss me.*

But we have to find Betty. She's been gone for almost a week. My raging hormones have to wait.

"I should go back to my dorm and regroup. We're close to finding Betty. I feel it," she says.

"Are you sure you're safe out there?" I ask.

She laughs. "Yeah, it's mostly paintballs and a few herrings being thrown. I'll dodge them."

She points to Carmilla's side of the room. "But what about you? You sure you'll be okay?" The smell of vanilla oil is so strong that I can't think of anything else. All I've got is a nod. Danny cracks open the door, checks the hall and waves goodbye.

"Take care," I manage.

Once I close and lock the door, I thump my forehead on it. "Oh my God. Take care? Really?" Not that my excruciating awkwardness is important in the middle of the mayhem on campus, but I can't get her out of my head.

Camera ready to go, time to catch my roommate in the act. I know it's early for Carmilla — it's only midnight. I don't expect her for hours but I need to be on alert — at least my camera does. I double-check for the umpteenth time.

I tuck myself in, falling asleep in seconds. When I wake up, I'm entangled in my covers, drenched in sweat. A glance at Carmilla's bed reveals that I'm alone. Doesn't look like she ever managed to come home. I wrap my blanket around my neck, whip up some hot chocolate and settle in to watch the footage from last night.

An empty bed. More empty bed. Zero movement. Much to my surprise and dismay, there's nothing incriminating there. Hours of nothing. How can this be? I was so certain I would catch her in some evil act.

I must have fallen asleep again, because I wake up with a start. Was I dreaming? There was something or someone in the room. I was so sure it was Carmilla. There was a noise under the bed, something prowling around on the floor. A dark face, then a little girl crying. I pulled the blankets over me to hide but the darkness started seeping through my blankets like blood. More and more until I was drowning in it.

I'm wide awake now and wishing I wasn't. Then I notice a sliver of my door open. The sound of wind is deafening.

The door slams shut.

• SEVEN •

It's day three with the mother of all night terrors whenever I try to sleep. The dream, more like a nightmare, is so specific that it haunts me. Maybe it's my steady diet of grape soda and Pop-Tarts? The dreams are frighteningly similar to the one Natalie had before she was snatched up. Am I next? Between lack of sleep and trying to figure out how Carmilla is involved with all the kids that have gone missing, I'm on edge all the time.

No, I'm full-on freaking out.

When Carmilla blows through the door, I nearly leap out of my skin.

"Jumpy much? What's the matter? Worried your girlfriend is out with the frat boys making it all nice again in the Silas world? Maybe she switched teams?"

"Danny's not my girlfriend. We're hanging out. She's just

cool. Unlike you." Shit, that wasn't nice. Carmilla looks like I kicked her. "Sorry, I've been having really freakish dreams."

"Dreams are supposed to be strange. Happens to me all the time. Like, last night, I dreamed that I was trapped under a bed," she admits, taking me completely off guard.

"Wait, you were under a bed?" My stomach is churning.

"A little girl was hovering above me crying," she continues. "Blood started raining down the edges of the bed frame until I drowned."

"So explicit," I squeak.

She brushes me off. "But just a dream. No need for all the twitchiness you've got going on."

How are we sharing the same nightmare, yet she can brush it off? I wrap the covers around me.

Carmilla grabs one of my doughnuts and takes it down in two bites. I've given up bitching about my food. I'm certain she does it on purpose to get a rise out of me.

"I'm not twitching." I'm totally twitching. It's all the sugar.

She gets next to me. "Hey. Not teasing you. Obviously this is affecting you. Listen, if you need something to help you sleep, I got your back. I can help you."

Is she being nice to me or setting me up to punk me? "That's sweet of you. And out of character, if I'm being honest."

"Don't get all Hallmark on me. I don't need you losing your shit in the middle of the night and going postal on me." She cackles on her way back out the door.

I flush. "Right. Right." Now she decides to be a halfway-decent human. Just my luck. The kidnapper is becoming my friend. Irony at its finest. Must keep my guard up.

LaFontaine pops in. "Where is she headed?"

I check my notes with her schedule on them. Spying is a full-time job. "Philosophy of Tyranny in the Robespierre Building." Not one light class in her course load. The more disturbing the better with this one.

Some quirky guy in a lab coat, carrying a clipboard, appears out of nowhere and blows something into our room. A dustlike cloud disperses.

"Oh my God, what was that?" I scream. *Maybe it's a drug that renders you helpless. Maybe they're going to kidnap us next,* I'm thinking. *Maybe we're all going to die.*

Casually, LaFontaine ducks. "Just a guy from the Alchemy Club. I think that was spores or something like it." I'm not sure I'm ever going to get used to Silas. "I'll shadow Carmilla. Keep an eye out." LaFontaine darts out after her, taking sleuthing to a whole new level.

I hear Perry yelling at LaFontaine. "This is insane! Stop this right now!" Perry is not on board with our roommate surveillance project, so the two of them have been on the rocks. Luckily, LaFontaine doesn't give up easily.

With the room to myself, I chug down almost my entire mug of coffee, not caring that it's scalding my mouth. I need to get through this footage and post a new update. All I can do is sigh when I see what my roommate has been up to when I'm in class. Per usual, helping herself to all of my food and drinks. I watch her holding a Luke Bryan CD that combusts in her hand. I have to rewatch that one a few times to make sure my eyes aren't playing tricks on me. I mean, not just the disintegrating disk but Luke Bryan? I would never have guessed she was a country music fan.

I break up my Pop-Tart and dump it in my coffee, spooning bites into my mouth as I view the video. Carmilla lifts her bed up over her head with superhuman strength, reaching underneath to grab a book. Okay, that's not normal.

She props herself up on the bed. I zoom in. What the hell? Is she reading my journal? Such a violation of privacy and the unspoken roommate code. I've got to get Betty back.

I watch her fill her soy milk container with a bloodlike substance, then shotgun it like a hungover rock star. She tissues off the residue on her lips, then swipes my new toothbrush off my dresser. I flip out when she uses it to clean the soles of her boots while she laughs, clearly amused at her disgusting antics.

I knew Silas was odd, but the people here are more than just weird. There's something ominous hanging in the air, and it's heaviest right here in our dorm room. Something is up with Carmilla and it's not good. Like, all signs point to her being the kidnapper.

Terrified, I know I need to post my update. I don't bother to change out of my pajamas or brush my hair. I run my fingers through it like a comb and get after it. Update time. *Remain calm*, I coach myself.

"Here's where we are with surveilling the roommate. She's nocturnal. She's never up before five o'clock in the afternoon, then she vanishes like a puff of smoke until daybreak. She eats nothing other than *my* chocolate and chugs that protein mess she keeps in the soy milk container. Also, the girl is a world-class slob."

I pause so I can down another cup of joe and take a breath.

"Silas is so peculiar. No doubt about that, but I'm fairly certain spontaneous combustion, Wonder Woman strength and an all-protein diet are unorthodox even for this place. Add that to Carmilla's familiarity with all the snatched girls ..."

Carmilla appears in the doorway, scaring the crap out of me.

"I'm not doing anything!" I screech, freaking out.

"Harry Potter cosplay on your screen again?" she teases.

I rush to close all the open tabs on my computer screen so she can't see that I'm posting another video about her. My fingers zip around the keyboard so quickly that I accidentally open a YouTube video. Music blasts.

"You listen to Beethoven?" she asks, moving closer to me and the computer screen.

"Surprise," I lie, pounding the keys until only my screen-saver remains.

She's standing there holding a bracelet that looks like a dried bat wing with red beads on it. It's black and feathery. Quite beautiful, if you like freaky bracelets.

"I brought you this — it will help you with your nightmares. It should drive them away," she murmurs so considerately that I think she's a different person. Like her body has been snatched by aliens. It could happen — especially here. She steps closer to me, taking my wrist in her hand. Her fingers are soft and warm. Unlike Danny's, Carmilla's scent is musky, more like a pine tree mixed with herbs. Watching her wrap the bracelet around my wrist, I'm in a trance. I think what I like most is that my roommate thought about me. Kind of nice for a change.

"For it to work, you need to wear it at all times. You're annoying and all, but if you burn out and I lose you, I'll probably end up with some freak for a roommate."

I'm not sure what transpires between us but something does. Enough that I boldly ask, "In the spirit of this new friendship, can I ask you a question?"

She gazes into my eyes. "You may."

Deep breath. Here goes nothing. "Where do you go all night?"

The smile spreads, her laugh maniacal. "A girl has to keep some things a secret. Don't you like a girl with some mystery?"

I think she's flirting with me. I've never been in this position in my life. Not one but two girls kind of giving me attention in a good way? There's something in the Silas air.

Carmilla opens the door. "Later, cutie."

I fall back on my bed, reviewing what just transpired between me and my not-so roommate from hell. Carmilla was concerned enough to bring me some sort of bat-wing bracelet that wards off evil, so she cares about something sinister befalling me. She got close to me, held my wrist for a lot longer than she needed to and cocked her head while she spoke to me. That falls under flirting. Even I got that. But what does it all mean? What if Carmilla is setting me up to be her next victim by luring me into a false sense of security? She's such a Slytherin.

I can't have this happening. I loosen the bracelet, empty out a plastic container of mini peanut butter cups and store it in there. Sliding it under my bed, I take down all, I mean every last one, of the peanut butter cups.

Perry knocks, then enters my room without waiting for a response. "Anything new?"

Show her or don't show her? Show her, for sure. "Just this." I cue up the footage and hit Play. Her eyes remain glued to the screen as she watches Carmilla lift her bed like it's just a few pounds. She gasps.

"Right?" I ask.

The next piece of footage is the exploding CD. Perry turns ashen. "She's a witch. We have to get you out of here. Now."

"I'm not going anywhere. This is where I live. This is my room. If anyone is going, it's her." Though now I know she's not all bad …

"Leave it alone, Laura, I'm begging you. I don't want anything to do with her or this. I'm all out. And don't involve LaFontaine," she warns before bolting through the door.

I still have the footage on Repeat, trying to make sense of the senseless.

LaFontaine pops their head in. "Sorry, we lost Carmilla at the Shunned House again after her class. Damn. This is killing my rep."

"She was just here."

"How the hell? She's slippery. What's up with you, Laura?" LaFontaine settles down next to me on the side of my bed.

"Everything. I miss my dad, even when he's riding me about my grades. I'm behind in my classes. I'm sucking at life." And my roommate may or may not have me next on the hit list. All signs point to me. My stomach tightens, as does my face. Fear will do that to you. What if I never see my family again?

"Talk to me," says LaFontaine.

"I think I'm next up on the victim list."

"You really think Carmilla has you in the crosshairs?"

I breathe in. "I want to be wrong but I'm not sure I am. Perry wants me to leave it alone. But I can't. You know what I mean?"

"For sure. I think Perry's wrong" — said with an impish smile — "we can go over her head."

"You'd do that?" I'm shocked that they would go around Perry.

"We have to."

I hesitate. "Who's even over her head?"

"The dean." Not her again.

"What would we even tell her? I get that Carmilla is doing some pretty outrageous things on the video, but the dean isn't a fan of my videos. Won't that get us in trouble?"

"Yes and no," LaFontaine explains. "If the dean wants to control Carmilla, who better to share our theories with? You have proof, so that helps the dean. You can use all of your cub reporter skills. I think we should go to the Faculty Club. She's there every afternoon."

They make a valid point but I'm hesitant. I need to think this through. "I thought we were avoiding her at all costs."

"Desperate times …"

I do feel desperate. "Let's do this!" Now I'm fired up.

LaFontaine holds up a finger. "You might want to consider a shower. No offense but you're ripe."

"Are you insinuating that I smell?" I use deodorant. I think I'm offended. No, I know I am.

"When was the last time you showered?"

I sniff my armpits and ponder the question before silently making my way to the shower. I can't argue with them on this. Something has to give when you're juggling crime solving and freshman first love. Not to mention Carmilla. And for me that thing has been personal hygiene. "Give me an hour, then we'll find the dean."

LaFontaine gives me a thumbs-up before leaving. Seriously, the shower drain is clogged with Carmilla's raven hair. I use a hanger to remove it. Disgusting.

I have to admit the hot water was just what I needed to reinvigorate my fighting spirit. LaFontaine and I devise a plan to sneak into the Faculty Club pretending to be a distinguished young visiting professor and a research assistant. LaFontaine has the blueprint of the building spread out on my table. "Here's the entrance. There's usually a greeter. We'll need these, just in case." A phony faculty badge with my picture on it is handed to me. Impressive.

"We need to dress the part," I say, a little panicked. My excitement might have got the best of me when LaFontaine suggested this. Maybe I should heed Perry's warning.

LaFontaine reaches inside a hefty bag and unearths a bougie blazer. "Here, wear this with some dark jeans. Pull your hair back. You'll look just like Ms. Brewster, the guest lecturer for modern European history."

I do as directed. I commit. LaFontaine slips on a sweater and jeans with some glasses and continues with the plan. "We'll walk through the courtyard into the lobby area. If anyone questions us, we'll whip out the badges."

Please do not let it come to that, I think. I'm already sweating.

"We'll mill about. Zero in on the dean. Move in. Unleash the truth. Then we're out. Five minutes tops."

Seems fairly innocuous. I try not to think about everything that could go wrong.

The Faculty Club is tucked away behind some trees on the north end of campus, near a man-made creek. The path to the

French doors is cobblestone, and the building is unmarked, like everyone just knows what it is. Like the rest of the campus, the Faculty Club is dark and foreboding.

Inside are leather couches and a dimly lit open space where at least twenty-five faculty members are drinking wine and socializing. We mingle, fitting in according to plan until LaFontaine gets baited into a conversation with the head of gnostic mathematics. One minute I'm eating a canapé, the next I'm getting pushed into a table. LaFontaine starts going all WWE on this professor, arguing about the long-term strategic plan for the Illuminati. They keep screaming that they're trying to raise awareness. Apparently LaFontaine subscribes to the notion that traditional religious ideas are no longer a belief system. That does not go over well. Apparently it's a hot-button topic for both of them.

LaFontaine lobs a melon ball at the professor. That's when the professor stabs LaFontaine with a skewer from the chicken kebab, cutting their face.

Campus police arrive, along with some curious students. Hysteria and yelling start. Punches fly, along with fish. It must be written somewhere that you throw fish during times of distress at Silas.

As we're being "removed," I snag a little something off the wall. It's a picture of the Dean's Council circa 1954, and I tuck it under my blazer quickly. With the wind blowing at fifty degrees, our teeth chattering more with each step we take, we head to the library to figure out who these people are in the photo with that era's dean. Research time.

One of them is a ringer for my roommate. But the picture was taken before she was born. Now we're on a mission.

We head across campus to the library. Mostly everyone is gone by the time we get there. LaFontaine and I tiptoe around, not wanting to call attention to ourselves. We hear an odd noise.

"Did you hear that?" I'm a little jumpy.

"Sounds like something scratching," LaFontaine says.

It weirds me out a little but we continue our journey, making our way to the subbasement. LaFontaine moves toward the online system to access the whereabouts of all the yearbooks from 1954 until now.

"Hey, the staircase moved. It's not here," I say. Chills run down my spine.

LaFontaine concentrates on the computers that begin to rattle. Then they get louder and louder. "Run. Run. Run," they warn us.

We both freeze. "What the hell?" I ask. The rumbling from stacks of books is getting closer and closer. Some of the books start flying at us, totally airborne. Right off the shelves.

We duck but not quickly enough. The card catalog attacks us, leaving paper-cut carnage on our arms and faces. We're stuck in a vortex of flying fiction and index cards from the seventies.

LaFontaine tries to fight them off, yelling, "They're vicious!" and swiping at the blood on their shirt.

"We have to do something!" I scream.

LaFontaine makes a flamethrower from hairspray and a lighter because, of course, they have those handy. Those bio classes are really paying off.

So basically we're trapped in a flaming vortex. Suddenly the sprinkler system goes off, soaking us. We snatch up a stack of yearbooks before they get drenched and climb out of a basement window, managing to evade the fire department and campus police who are converging.

But we've found a gold mine.

•

We dodge all the commotion and race back to my dorm room. Perry is livid when we get there but tends to our wounds. Yeah, wounds.

"What happened?" she asks.

"Things got nasty after the altercation with security at the Faculty Club. These paper cuts are a bitch," I complain. LaFontaine is brooding, still reeling from the professor's verbal lashing as well as the conflagration.

"Didn't I say leave it alone?" Perry shouts.

"We had to go," I insist. "We've come this far."

"It was irresponsible," Perry snaps. "I'm not doing this

anymore. I won't watch you all be the next in line."

Danny is mad in a more subdued way, pacing in front of the window on the lookout.

"Ow," LaFontaine complains when Perry dabs the skewer puncture with alcohol.

All the arguing in front of the webcam — which stays on all of the time now — isn't really helping, but the students of Silas need to know the truth. They need to know what happened when we pursued our lead.

"Do I need to remind you that if you were minding your own business and leaving this alone just as we discussed, you wouldn't be yelping right now?" Perry says in frustration.

Dejected, LaFontaine nods.

"Yeah," I interject, "but as they were dragging us out, I snatched this picture off the wall. Security never saw us. Check it out."

I wave the photo in front of Danny. "This is the Dean's Council in, like, 1954. Look at the woman in the black dress. Maybe Carmilla's grandmother or something?"

LaFontaine tries to explain to Perry. "There was only one way to find out who these people are. That's why we went to the library."

Perry passes around mugs of hot cocoa, her anger subsiding as her motherly instinct takes over.

I slide next to Danny, stringy wet hair and all, leaving the emergency blanket wrapped around me. I open the yearbooks. "Look at all these names," I say. "Basically, the same girl shows up every twenty years. It's my roommate, Carmilla. With a new name, like no one has ever heard of an anagram."

Danny takes the sheet of paper and reads the names off: "Millarca Kersantin 1994, Arcillma Karstienn 1974, Mircalla Karnstein 1954. Not very inventive, if you ask me."

Next to each name is a picture of Carmilla. Carmilla 1994 is sporting a sexy schoolgirl look with a short tartan skirt and an undersized sweater. Carmilla 1974 rocks a dressy pair of flared pants with a skintight ribbed white tank that makes me do a double take. The 1950s look is much more conservative. Long skirt with a short-sleeved shirt buttoned at the neck.

Truth: she looks amazing no matter the year.

"The thing is, every time this person shows up, students go missing," Danny says.

"We already know that Carmilla is nocturnal and has the strength of an ape. She's lived forever and she drinks blood and she doesn't age," I explain.

LaFontaine gets excited. "Well, we know she's a vampire. We've known that since the first milk situation."

I leap to my feet and throw my hands up. "Hold up. All of you knew Carmilla was a vampire? A straight-up blood-sucking vampire?" I can't believe this.

"You didn't know?" LaFontaine scoffs.

Danny speaks up. "I had no idea either. I just thought she was a bitch."

"She's not a vampire," Perry philosophizes. "There are

no such things. She's just got amazing skin, hates light and is hemoglobin deficient."

Even she knows she sounds ridiculous. Of course Carmilla is a vampire. That explains a lot, right? How could I have missed it? All the signs were there. This college is turning me into a clueless idiot. I flash to her biting poor Kirsch. Did she make him a vampire, too?

I grab LaFontaine by the shoulders. "Let me get this straight. We've got something lurking around campus taking people, and you didn't think it was pertinent information to share that my roommate is a vampire?"

"Well, when you put it that way …"

I start freaking out. "I'm next. The creepy dreams, the charm bracelet. It all means something." I'll never sleep again.

"And her seductive eyes. The way she looks at you, it's so obvious that she's crushing on you," LaFontaine throws in.

On you? I wonder. *You as in everyone? Or you as in me?*

A vampire who's crushing on me. Is that even possible?

Danny's head snaps back. "What seductive eyes?" I almost make a joke but she's straight-up serious. She's jealous.

"Come on, Danny, you've seen her," says LaFontaine. "She's stunning. Her hair flows like a majestic horse's mane. Her dark eyes look right through you."

I have to put a stop to this — we're veering off course. "You guys. She. Is. A. Vampire. Oh God, I'm living with Lestat. How are we supposed to stop a vampire?"

"Staking. Decapitation. Immolation," Danny reads off her phone. Google knows all. "Something about an iron needle through the heart. Normally, I wouldn't condone this kind of thing, but in cases of seductive eyes I could make an exception."

Perry holds up her hand. "Stop! We can't just kill everyone that Sue, I mean, LaFontaine, thinks might be a supernatural creature. Only loony tunes make plans to stake someone with no real proof."

"Ha! We have so much proof. Who wants some soy milk? Why, I do, I'm feeling anemic." LaFontaine thinks the joking is hilarious, but no one is laughing. An awkward silence hangs in the air.

I have to weigh in. "She's right, guys. Even if we figure out a way to turn Carmilla into a firepit, that would mean we'd never get the answers we've been searching for. And we'd have no shot at finding Betty or Elsie. We don't need her dead … or deader. We need answers."

Danny puts her hand on my knee. "Okay, Hollis. How do we trap a vampire?" I wish I knew the answer. Also, I wish I knew if I wanted her to keep her hand there.

"You're not going to like this but I have a brilliant idea," LaFontaine offers. Perry cringes. "We use something to lure her into a trap of some kind — a rope net, maybe, or a room filled with garlic. That's the easy part."

"Okay," says Danny, ready to go this far. "What's the bait? Bags of blood?"

Matter-of-factly, LaFontaine replies, "More like, who's the bait?" then looks at me. "Laura."

How did I know that was coming? Danny stands between me and LaFontaine.

"Absolutely not."

Perry paces nervously around the room, pulling her hair in and out of a ponytail. She's waiting for someone to say something.

So I speak up. "I'm down with it, I think."

Danny turns to me, taking my arm. "Explain to me how offering yourself up on a platter to a vampire who wants to seduce you isn't the worst idea ever?" She almost sounds betrayed.

I edge close to her. "I know this isn't the smartest plan but it's the only plan."

"Hollis, the fact that it's a default plan isn't good enough!" Danny insists.

"Are we still belaboring the vampire theory?" Perry asks. "It's probably just some Silas crackpot jerking us around."

"I'll bring salt with me," I promise Danny. "Wait, is salt a vampire thing?"

"Not unless we're making margaritas," LaFontaine cracks, attempting to lighten the mood. Lucky for me, just then Kirsch and Will stumble in with Sarah Jane and Natalie. The girls dance into the room chanting, "Party! Party!" I can't help chuckling at the grass skirts and leis they are wearing.

Kirsch talks over them. "Hey, Laura's friends. Will and I came to invite you to a luau tomorrow night. A celebration of peace." He singles Danny out. "It's what you wanted, right? Peace. So you need to come." He bounces in, wearing a coconut bra, goofy as all hell. "We're even roasting a pig with an apple in its mouth."

The mismatched socks and camo cargo shorts clash with the bra. That doesn't stop him from posing for selfies. He checks his latest picture. "Posting."

Of course he is. His phone starts to sing with dings from all of his followers.

I nod, leaning close to him. "Question. If we were going to try to catch the person who's been inflicting all this chaos on us, would you and your brothers be in on it with us? You know, to help me out." I know he'd never say no to me.

"We'd be honor bound to shred that guy for you," he answers. He bows. Will and Danny shake their heads, but I'm starting to think his goofy is charming. Or it's the sleep deprivation mixing with the fear that's distorting things.

"Great. We'll see you at the party, right, ladies?"

They all grudgingly grunt yes or various forms of it.

"God, they're such tools," Danny whispers.

Perry chimes in. "Anything but a Zeta party. Last time we went to one, they pantsed Kirsch in front of everyone."

"So immature," Danny says.

I put my foot down. "We need their help. We're going. And we're going to like it."

Perry drags LaFontaine out of my room, lecturing them on why all of this is the worst idea and a waste of time since vampires aren't real. "You're buying into the fiction of it all. Tom Cruise does not make them real."

Once they leave, Danny implores, "Please don't do this. I have a bad feeling. I don't want anything to happen to you."

Don't look into her eyes, I tell myself. "I know you aren't psyched about me teaming up with the Zetas, but if I'm vampire bait I need numbers to have my back. Having a band of 'roid ragers on my side doesn't seem like such a bad thing."

I can't believe my first semester in college has come to this. I am vampire bait. I need the Zetas. Two truths I never thought would be.

"That's hard to argue with, but I'm still not a fan of it. Dangling you out there for her and knowing we're relying on the Zetas does not help. Get some rest. We'll talk in the morning and figure this out together."

Concern is written all over Danny's face, and her feet drag on her way out the door. As she leaves, I hear her mutter, "Seductive. I'll show her."

•

I sit down at my computer with a bag of candy, racking my brain for ways to lure Carmilla into the trap we set. I guess I could get bitten. Not liking that one. What would Mina Harker do? She'd totally act alluring and sexy and get chomped on. I remind myself that I'm not Mina.

I thumb through a stack of books for ideas. *Dracula*, not bad, I like it. *The Vampire Lestat*, a favorite. *Twilight*, just no. Bella putting Edward so high up on a pedestal, being her be all and end all. The damsel in distress. So 1950s. Dog-tired, I drift off, head planted on my forearm across the desk.

I startle awake, clutching my neck and mumbling, "Black as the Pit, and terrible … terrible." I rub my eyes, focusing on a shadow on my windowsill. It's Carmilla, smoking a cigarette, smoke rings billowing above her.

"You're here?"

She turns to me, her regal profile all mine to see. Hair flowing past her slight shoulders, covering a tight white T-shirt. The moonlight falling perfectly over her.

"Been here awhile. You were having another bad dream. At least it sounded like that." Her voice is soft. Like she cares.

"Yeah. I can't seem to escape them. What are you doing?"

"Counting the stars. So beautiful. Tranquil. It's so comforting. To think of how tiny we are in comparison. All the lives we've led, the people who've crossed our paths."

"You really are a philosophy major," I crack. Though now I know she really has lived in other times.

She drifts my way. "I think your unconscious wants you to give up the vlog and get to your lit paper."

"Huh?"

"You were dreaming about the Kipling book you said was on your reading list."

"You remembered," I say, surprised.

"One of my all-time favorites. 'Black as the Pit, and terrible as a demon, was Bagheera.' I've always loved that. So beautiful it makes you cry."

The depth of her words and the way she articulates them almost suck me in. I see pain behind Carmilla's eyes and feel her tortured soul. It's speaking to me, in poetry. *Stop listening*, my inner good judgment tells me.

"Dangerous as well. You know, giant black cat and all," I say. She gets closer. I feel her breath. I fall into her eyes. "Hey, the Zetas are having a party," I continue. "I know we had a rocky start, but how about if we go together and hang out. Look at the stars."

She's an inch from my lips, then I almost feel hers graze mine. "I think I might like that very much."

Oh no. This is going to be harder than I thought.

It's her eyes.

· EIGHT ·

My bed is closet carnage as I search for the perfect outfit to bait a vampire. I hold up a tank top, supertight. Not me. Next up, a midriff top with short shorts. Too obvious. I put my favorite plaid pajama bottoms on and check myself out in the mirror. I'm definitely comfy but don't think it'll do the trick. I try a sexy dress. Flowy, white. Neck and shoulders on display. Over the top? Probably, but I'm owning it.

Danny walks through the open door. (I finally gave up worrying about locking the door since everyone pretty much treats this place like a subway station.) "I brought you some liquid courage," she offers, handing me some tequila. She puts her phone in her pocket and just looks at me. "Is that what you're wearing?" she asks.

I'm self-conscious as all hell so this isn't helping. "Not sexy enough?"

She gets her flirt on. "That is not the problem. You're totally working the brooding lover thing. You could really tone it down. You know?"

I'd like to yell, *No, I don't. Just speak the words so I know if we are a thing or not.* I know fighting vampires doesn't lend itself to romance, but I'd like to know where I stand before I go into battle. Instead, I keep quiet about that and go somewhere else. "Wanna hear my plan?"

"I'm all ears. But damn, you look amazing. Makes me wish I was a vampire," she flirts. Yes, this might be a thing. Just not right this second.

"We're going to hit the luau for a bit. Have a drink or two to loosen her up, get her off her game. I'll ask her to go for a walk, then the Zetas will grab her. Fingers crossed she doesn't ingest me first. That's the plan."

"Just be careful, please. Text me as soon as they have her. I worry about you." I can't get derailed by her lavender smell or her perfect hair. *Stop it, Laura. Focus.*

"Promise," I assure her before she leaves.

Back to my makeup. I add some black eyeliner and soft pink lipstick, then spray some dry shampoo in my hair to give it a tousled, sexy look. Or something like that.

Carmilla sneaks in. "Don't you look like a virgin sacrifice," she purrs. I turn to see my vampire roommate in a corset and leather pants, with a bottle of champagne and two glasses.

"I'm not the one wearing a corset. Which is … wow."

Carmilla fills the glasses. She is flat-out the most beautiful person who has ever been in my sphere. She is intoxicating. Vampire or not.

"What's happening here?" I ask, trying not to show that I'm about to faint.

She hands me a glass, gets close. "The more I thought about a bonfire with those morons and a roasted pig, the less appealing it sounded. Parties are for new beginnings, glowing possibility. So I brought the party here."

She's good. I sip the champagne, checking out the bottle. It looks super expensive. "Where did you even get this?"

She raises her eyes. "I have my ways. There was champagne at the first party I went to," she shares, edging closer to me.

"You say it like it was a hundred years ago."

She reaches for my wrist, running her fingers from the crease in my elbow down to my hand. Her touch feels like cashmere. Softer than soft. "You aren't wearing your bracelet. If you don't have it on, it can't protect you."

Does she mean I'm not protected from her, or from someone else? My head is a muddled mess. "Oh yeah. Right." She's unnerving me. I can't pinpoint what I'm feeling. I just know it's a lot of unknown.

Her sweetness fades. "If you didn't like it, you should have just said so," she says like I hurt her feelings.

"No, no. I do like it. I like it a lot." Her tenderness flusters me. Maybe I'm reading too much into this, but I think this is a big deal to her. Like she truly wants me safe. I'm not sure if I can go through with the plan now. Time to call for reinforcements. I reach in my pocket for my phone, but Carmilla nabs it.

"I was just going to text Danny and the girls," I explain. "Bring the party here. Like you said."

Carmilla tosses my phone on the bed. "Maybe I don't feel like sharing right now." She closes in on me all suggestive-like.

"That almost sounded flattering, but you made it sound like I'm a snack or something." Really, I'm not sure I can do this.

That comment seems to strike a funny bone. Her howling gets deeper and longer. "You're wound so tight. I should know better than to get involved. But there's something about you, Laura Hollis, that I can't resist."

"My fashion sense?"

She leans in alarmingly close, cups my chin. "Definitely not that." She's either going to kiss me or bite me. I ready myself for either. As her lips inch closer to mine, I lick mine nervously.

Her warm breath tickles my face. Those eyes take hold of mine and don't let go. Like it or not, I'm drawn to Carmilla and I want her to kiss me. I consider making the first move, then chicken out. She's moving in now.

It's on.

Just as it's about to happen, someone kicks the door in. Did Carmilla lock it?

"What are you doing? Get away from her!" Danny screams, yanking Carmilla away from me.

"What the hell?" Carmilla yells right back.

LaFontaine rushes in. "Get her, boys!" In a flash, I see Kirsch karate-chop Carmilla, then Will knock her to the floor. They hold her down while Danny ties her hands and feet with ropes at lightning speed. LaFontaine flies across the room. Will jumps up and puts duct tape across Carmilla's mouth. Kirsch adds a garlic necklace along with a slew of crosses draped on her. It happens so fast, all the flailing limbs, the swinging fists, the shouting voices. The whole time, my heart is pounding against my chest. I should have aborted the mission. This is all wrong. My brain is in a blender with all of my feelings.

When the dust settles, I can't believe my eyes. Our room looks like a full-on hurricane blew through and left a wake of mass destruction. The mattresses are upended. Danny's eye is swollen, turning shades of purple, and Perry is cowering in the corner clutching a cross. A cross.

I rush to Danny's side, checking her eye. "Are you okay?" I look over her shoulder at Carmilla. Something in my chest tugs at me. Hard.

"Better now. I knew she had you trapped." She did this for me. I can barely look at her. I was about to kiss Carmilla and she was trying to save me. I feel terrible. So conflicted.

"My gut told me this was the time," she continues. "It was like I could sense you needing me. That's why we rushed in."

Feeling worse.

Danny turns around to Carmilla. "Your plan didn't work."

Carmilla is steaming. Epically pissed off.

"If anyone cares, I think I'm bleeding," LaFontaine says. "Something hit me on the side of my head. It hurts. Help. Anyone?"

"Did anyone see where the Zetas went?" I inquire.

LaFontaine manages to answer. "Those idiots stepped over me to get back to their party. Kirsch was mumbling about getting a pig sandwich before it was gone."

"So we're stuck with the fallout?" Perry asks, pointing to Carmilla.

I can't focus on my confusion. I have a job to do, and I promised myself I would see this through no matter what. I can't let her eyes distract me. Again.

I adjust the camera to get Carmilla directly in the webcam's eye. "Time for a party, Silas. We've got our vampire. No more of her flirting with unsuspecting girls or hunting them down. It's over. We win. Now we just need to un-pod Nat and SJ then find Betty and Elsie."

Okay, we still have a lot to do.

I'm scared to look at Carmilla. I steal a glance and don't like what's looking back. It's betrayal. I got caught up in the heat of the moment with her. A moment that never should have happened. Anyone sucked into her eyes would have done the same thing.

Wouldn't they?

Perry applies an ice pack to an angry lump on the side of

LaFontaine's head. LaFontaine winces. "That hurts." I swear Perry presses harder.

"Now what?" I ask.

Carmilla is spitting nails, red-hot mad. She's trying to wiggle out of the ropes so hard that the chair scrapes along the floor. Her grunts are getting louder and angrier.

Danny gets up in her face. "This was so worth it. How does it feel to be trapped like those girls you took?"

Carmilla jerks her head back and forth.

I settle my hand on Danny's shoulder to encourage her to leave Carmilla alone. When my eye catches Carmilla's, she turns away.

I don't like the way that hurts.

A bloodcurdling scream and a rumbling from outside stun us all into stone-cold silence.

"What the hell was that?" I ask.

"Can't be anything good," LaFontaine answers.

Kirsch rushes in, carrying a half-eaten sandwich. "Come quick. I think someone tried to take Natalie, and Sarah Jane's not breathing. I think she might be dead."

"Oh my God," I say. "That can't be. We have the vampire. There's just no way."

Maybe he's drunk.

Carmilla growls.

"We need help," Kirsch squeals. "We have to find Natalie." He takes a bite of his sandwich.

"Someone has to stay with her," Danny snarls.

Perry points to Carmilla. "She's not going anywhere." The ropes are so tight that her knuckles are turning white.

"Dudes, come on!" Kirsch yells.

We race across the moonlit campus to the Zeta House. The lawn is littered with empty plastic cups and it reeks of stale beer. The DJ is still rocking the party that's in full swing in spite of the fact that Sarah Jane is motionless near the firepit. The pig on the spit eyeing us makes the creep factor multiply. LaFontaine checks Sarah Jane's pulse.

But it's too late.

· NINE ·

We trudge back to my room, all somber. This is quite a predicament. Carmilla couldn't have done this. It's impossible — she's been restrained for hours.

"I just don't get it. All the signs were there. They were pointing directly to Carmilla. No question. Sarah Jane shouldn't be …" I know my voice is cracking. I'm on the verge of tears. Perry pats me on the back. If we were wrong, and it seems like we were, then I did a horrible thing to Carmilla. I lift an eye toward her and she snarls before turning away.

Fair.

We 100 percent screwed this up.

Danny dashes in, waving two index cards.

"These were in their rooms on their beds. It's the exact same drivel that was on your card. Same muck stuck to them as was on the one left for you. It's all connected somehow."

LaFontaine shadows Danny with a pair of test tubes. "I'll take some samples. We'll figure out exactly what this sludge is."

Danny is thinking out loud. "Someone kidnapped Sarah Jane and Natalie, right? But why a second time? Why go through the trouble of giving them back, then kidnap them all over again?" Not to mention killing one of them.

Kirsch walks over. "I don't understand that either. It was supposed to be fun. We had beer pong and everything." I almost feel sorry for him. He's all about the party.

Out of nowhere, he lunges at Carmilla, grabbing her neck. "Why would you do this to her?"

We all leap to stop him, but it's Danny who pries him off Carmilla. "She wasn't there, Kirsch. She's been tied up here for the last few hours. It's not her."

Carmilla screams through her duct tape. I can't even look at her. This is all my fault.

Kirsch backs off, chilling out. "Thanks, Summer Psycho. I'm just freaking out about Sarah Jane. I liked her. I need to be with my bros."

I reach for his elbow. "Hang on, the bros can wait. We have to figure out why this is all happening."

"Let's review. One dead girl. One captured vampire," LaFontaine says.

"Now what?" I ask.

Carmilla shifts around in her chair, banging it on the floor to get our attention.

LaFontaine checks her out. "This is a bit of a dilemma we're in."

"I never wanted to kidnap anyone," Perry snaps. "This is a monumental mess. I think I'm breaking out in hives."

I state the obvious. "We need to untie her, Danny."

"What if she's involved somehow?" Danny says.

LaFontaine is on Danny's side. "I'd like to point out that it took six of us to subdue her and she still seems pissed off so I'm not in favor of unleashing the beast."

"It's not her!" I insist.

"Pretty sure it's illegal to hold someone hostage," Perry points out.

"I could take her to the bio lab. I bet there's all kinds of things we could learn with a little probing here and there. Blood work. Standard stuff." No one jumps on LaFontaine's bandwagon. "Or maybe she could answer a few questions or something."

"Look, this is my doing," I say. "I'll take care of it. She's our only lead. I'm not letting her out of my sight. I'm keeping her here with me."

Carmilla glares at Danny.

"We'll wait it out until she tells us what's going on," I continue. "Stay focused. We have to Girl the Hell Up. If we get caught, it's on me. What's the worst they can do? Expel me? At this point, that doesn't sound half bad."

LaFontaine, Perry and Danny rally around me as I roll Carmilla closer to us. She's still refusing to make eye contact with me, but I force the situation by kneeling in front of her. "We know you're a vampire. Don't bother denying it. We saw the pictures of you with each of the girls at the parties. You've been stalking all of them. So where are they?"

Silence.

I go at her again. "The sooner you tell us the truth, the better. What do you have to say for yourself?"

Nothing.

"You might want to take the duct tape off her mouth," LaFontaine says, chuckling.

Crap. I rip the tape off her mouth in an attempt to be a badass, but I really don't mean to yank that hard and it has to hurt like hell. Everyone winces along with Carmilla, and I come so close to apologizing but have to stick to the badass of it all if we're going to get Betty back. Carmilla works her jaw to stave off the hurt.

I try a kinder approach. "So, Carm, how did someone go missing and another get murdered when we've got you tied up with us?"

"Because I didn't have anything to do with it, you idiots. The person you all are hunting is still out there. You're wasting your time." Is she baring her teeth, or is that my imagination?

I'm safe as long as she's still tied up. Danny paces around her. "Do you think we're dumb enough to take your word for it? That you're truly innocent just because you say so?"

"Be logical. If I were a vampire, do you think I'd just sit here tied up?"

It's a fair point, but LaFontaine isn't giving an inch. "That's exactly what a sneaky vamp would do."

When Carmilla thrashes around, Perry says, "We need more rope, maybe zip ties. I saw that on *Law & Order*."

LaFontaine grabs the zip ties and adds them to the arsenal of rope and duct tape already securing Carmilla. One after another.

Zip.

Zip.

Zip.

It's the last zip tie around her wrists that cracks her.

"Fine. It's true, I am a vampire. It doesn't take a genius to confirm that. But I didn't touch those two girls. I was here with Laura. Alone."

Danny flinches.

Carm is pleased with herself when she sees Danny boiling mad. "Then I got ambushed by the frat toddlers and Red."

If looks could kill, Danny just took Carmilla out.

"The Zetas practiced karate on my ribs and legs. LaFontaine here was swinging a blender at me while the rest of you knocked me to the floor and dogpiled me. Or don't you remember that?"

I curl my lip. "What about an accomplice? A vampire in training or something?"

"You've met me? Do I seem like I play well with others?"

Fine. I've had it with this. "If you aren't snacking on these girls, then why are you stalking them?"

"Oh, aren't you cute? I don't have to stalk anyone. I get plenty of invitations. I'm popular." Voice dripping with all the sexy. *Ignore it, Hollis*, I plead with myself.

"You're a vampire."

"But not a kidnapper. Big difference, cupcake."

I turn to the others. "What are we going to do with her? She just admitted that she is a vampire. She could kill us all."

"If I wanted to do that, you wouldn't be here right now. Believe me. I'm a lover, not a fighter." She directs that last sentence right to me. My cheeks are on fire.

Perry speaks up. "That's insane. There's no such thing as a vampire. This is all Stephenie Meyer's fault. We could call Student Health Services. They're loaded up with meds. We can't keep her here. Can we?"

"Sure we can." I'm bound and determined to get through to her. I just can't look into her eyes or I'll be toast. There's no way that she doesn't have the answers we're looking for. If she didn't take the girls, she knows who did. She has to.

The lights flicker. What the hell?

"Are you going to help us or not?"

Her silent glare is my answer.

· TEN ·

For the last week, we've been taking turns babysitting Carmilla so that each of us can catch some sleep and make it to a few classes. I untie her when she's on my watch, since I have the guilties from the whole takedown plan.

I still can't get her to talk to me. I offered her my cookies and she snubbed me. She's dug in her heels and isn't giving in. Not one single word. I guess I can't blame her but I'll keep trying anyway. Being nice to her makes me feel better about how horribly I treated her.

It's day seven and Carmilla still isn't giving us any information, her lips solidly pressed together. Not even water could get through. Either she can really keep a secret or she's a glutton for punishment. The ropes lie on the floor next to her. I catch her rubbing her wrists.

She's appearing a little worse for the wear, if you ask me. Her skin is so pale that it's almost translucent. Her head flops to the side. I really do feel for her. She's so helpless.

"If you tell me what we want to know, I'll give you a sip of blood," I tell her. LaFontaine stocked the fridge. "Carm?"

She doesn't say a word.

A knock on the door distracts me. Danny and Perry rush to open it and block the view of Carmilla from whoever's there. There's been a steady stream of her admirers loitering in the hallway outside our room since she's gone MIA from the party circuit. She's right about one thing. She's quite popular.

"No, she hasn't come back," I hear Danny lie. She slams the door. Danny shoots me an exasperated look.

I whirl around toward Carmilla. "I know you left a trail of broken hearts in your wake, but any more of your one-night stands shows up, I'm going to start spraying them with water like stray cats."

No response. She glazes over, then her neck gives way, her chin hits her chest. Shit. Her eyes are rolling in her head.

"Carm!" I panic, then rush to the fridge and grab a blood bag, placing it in her mouth and squeezing lightly. Nothing happens.

"Drink it. I don't want you to die, Carmilla." This is not part of the plan! Carmilla coughs and her cheeks pink up.

"Thank God. Let me help you sit up. Would you like some more?" She looks so forlorn that my heart aches for her. She sips again, becomes more alert.

"Where did you manage to score that?" she whispers.

"LaFontaine got it from the campus hospital. She told them she needed it for some experiment in bio lab. There's more. Just in case." I spot some blood dripping form the corner of her mouth. I take my thumb and gently clear it away. Our eyes meet once more. Carmilla flinches, jerking away from me.

"Look, the humiliation of being held captive by a bunch of imbeciles for something I didn't do is plenty to deal with. I don't need you to make matters worse by wiping away my drool like I'm an infant."

I soften. "Just trying to help."

"It's not working."

"Carm, if you weren't involved, then why did it seem like you were about to eat me the night we captured you?"

"Hold up. You thought that was me trying to eat you? Not so much."

"If you weren't going to eat me …" Oh God. It was what I thought it was. "I'm not so good at reading people."

"Obviously, or I wouldn't be in this situation," she cracks.

I smile. "So you really were hitting on me?"

Carmilla's face heats up. "And you were luring me into a trap. Stake me now. It would be much less mortifying than this conversation. Talk about mixed signals."

Talk about awkward. Danny and Perry slink out the door, and I wish I could go with them, but I have to find a way to make things right with Carmilla.

I gather myself together and take a different approach. Because I want to. "Carm, how are we supposed to believe you if you don't tell us your side of the story? I want to believe you, I really do. Help me help you."

I hope my hand on hers assures her I really mean it.

Carmilla breathes deeply for a few moments and then it's like she just gives in. "Buckle up, cream puff. I'll tell you my side of the story. If you're ready."

"All buckled up. Let's get you in front of the camera." I wheel her next to the webcam, brush her hair. She's a hot mess. I mean, as messy as someone so gorgeous could be. Her mess is like most people's barely rumpled look. In this case, the loss of blood gives her a ghostlike glow that I find achingly attractive.

"This pathological need you have to document every little thing borders on obsessive," Carmilla says. The blood is helping. She's back.

"Here we go. It's your chance to convince the student body and us that you didn't have Betty for a snack."

Carmilla starts rattling off her life story in such a monotone that I almost doze off. "I was born Mircalla, daughter of Count Karnstein, in Styria, a duchy of Austria, in the year 1680. Austria was plagued by repeated invasions by the Ottoman Empire, but such things meant little to a wealthy girl, except that the princes who came to my father's estate wore uniforms that glittered with military honors. When I was eighteen, I attended a ball where I was murdered. By a vampire. That's it in a nutshell. How's that?"

"Boring. Let's make it exciting — do a … sock puppet show," I suggest. I need to keep the viewers engaged, and these last few minutes were more like taking a Xanax.

"You are certifiable, Hollis."

I rummage through the room to set up a makeshift stage. A sock on each arm, I start with the pink sock. "This is you. 'Oh, I love dancing, I love balls …'" Carmilla can't help lightening up. A black sock is the vampire. I attack the pink sock with the black one. "'I am a vampire. I am going to eat you.'" I growl like a monster.

Carmilla is amused. Who wouldn't be? I roll off the vampire sock, swapping it for a yellow-and-green one. "'Get up, beautiful lady.'" I hover over the Carmilla pink sock. I lift it and say, "'No way, I'm a vampire. I get to sleep all day.'"

Carmilla's laugh is infectious. She continues, "The whole wide world was opened up before me in death as it never was in life. My mother hosted grand balls every night with the finest food and drink. She made sure we had the most gorgeous gowns. We danced in the mirrored hall of Versailles. We watched the birth of a new world in philosophy, science and progressive ideas."

This explains her infatuation with philosophers and all of the parties. It's who she is.

Now I'm the one who's mesmerized. By her storytelling, her

cunning, her beauty. I'm falling under her spell all over again. I get up and dance around the room with sock puppets on my arms as she relates her tale.

"Every twenty years, we returned to Silas. The college was home to a long line of vampires, including my mother. Every twenty years we came back to perform a strange game that involved capturing five girls. Mother would arrange for me to befriend a young girl. She'd set it up so I was left behind at a ball and counted on me being taken in by a kind stranger and his daughter or niece. It worked every time."

I'm captivated.

"The girl and I would become inseparable. That's when dear old Mom would work her magic and the girl would suddenly get sick. She'd start to exhibit strange behavior, not acting like herself."

"Sounds familiar ..." I say. Same pattern here.

"It made them easy prey. Then, I would take them to my mother. Once my mother was ready, we'd start the cycle all over again. Until there were five."

I cease dancing. That's a lot to comprehend. "You're not exactly making a great case for yourself right now. You delivered these girls to your mother and never saw them again? Sounds like kidnapping to me." What did her mother even do with them? I wonder.

Carm interrupts my thoughts. "I was never the abductor. I was the lure. That's how I met Ell. In 1872." I note a change in her voice. Sorrow sneaks in. "All I wanted to do was sail to New York City to see the Metropolitan Museum of Art. It had just opened and I longed to visit, but Mother was a stickler for the game. The game began as it always did. An unsuspecting girl and her father offered me shelter when I was abandoned. A fast friendship formed. Only this time nothing was a lie. I cared about Ell. Deeply."

I use the socks to get to the truth. "'Oh, my heart beats only for you. I will not let you go. I love you.' 'I love you more.'" The socks wrestle. I'm sure I appear and sound like an idiot, but this is getting deep.

Carmilla's voice goes low. "When it came time for me to take Ell to my mother, I couldn't give her up. I planned our escape and went ahead of her to make all of the necessary arrangements."

It's alarming to hear her so vulnerable, so I try to keep things light. I flail a sock around. "'Life will be so much bigger than you ever imagined. Theater, concerts, the freedom to be ourselves.'"

Carmilla forges ahead, racked with pain. "Before Ell could join me, it happened. Disaster struck. My mother got to her first and told her that I was the one luring girls and then killing them. Ell believed her and told her all our secrets, along with my well-thought-out plan. Then she led my mother right to me. The price for my disobedience was to watch Ell be taken to her doom. After, my mother had me sealed in a coffin filled with blood so that I would waste my long centuries in the dark."

That revelation sends my sock puppets crashing to my sides.

Suddenly my dad doesn't seem so bad at all. I reach for Carmilla's shaking hand.

"I rotted under the earth for decades, until the war. When the war ended, so did my punishment, and I walked off the battlefield in Austria to meet the twentieth century. Bonus of being a vampire, we don't die unless you stake us. My mother found me in Paris in the early 1950s and didn't have the heart to reinter me. She figured I was of more use to her at Silas University. She made me leave Paris to help her once more. The details changed but the game did not. I was to meet girls on campus, make friends. Then my mother did with them as she saw fit. Whatever that was."

I stand up. "So nothing changed for you?"

"It did. This time I only pretended to play along. I ruined opportunities every chance I could, sending girls back to safety. The little revenges I got on my mother were sweet. I never knew what she did with the girls once they were taken, so I decided to bide my time until I learned the truth about what I had been a part of for so long."

That's why Sarah Jane and Natalie returned the first time. Carm intervened before her mother could lead them to their demise. The girls in my footage weren't her victims — she was actually thwarting her mother's attempts to kidnap them.

I'm stunned. "So you've been helping girls escape, not kidnapping them?" I really had this all wrong.

"You got it, cream puff," she says, pointing at me.

I have to ask, "Did you help Betty?"

"I wish I had. She was never on my list of students to befriend."

I sigh. "So someone Betty knew — someone she thought was a friend — was in fact a vampire. And they kidnapped her for your mother before you could help her?"

She nods.

There's still hope, then. "We'll just find your mother and get the missing kids back before they end up as dinner."

Carmilla bursts into uncontrollable laughter. "My mother will scoop your eyeballs out and serve them in martinis. You're already petrified of her."

She's obviously delirious. "I haven't even met your mother, so I can't be afraid of her."

Carm cocks her head. "Yes, you have. My mother is the dean."

· ELEVEN ·

In light of all of the revelations last night, Danny, Perry, LaFontaine and I are weighing the merits of releasing Carmilla. She made a compelling argument that she was only an accessory to the crimes — I mean, I'm convinced. But still, she did participate in tricking girls so her mother could dine on them or do whatever she does.

Perry is adamant. "Laura, we have to let her go. If the dean finds out we're holding a hostage, do you know how much trouble we can get in? She can take away my floor monitor status."

Girls are missing. Another is dead. The dean's a full-on killer with a posse of killer vampires.

"That's what you're worried about?" LaFontaine asks.

"I worked hard to get here, " Perry snarls.

Danny jumps in. "We can't let her go until we have a plan."

"If you want to go after the dean, have at it," Carmilla says. "I'll be just fine here binge-watching *Orange Is the New Black*. Fair warning. You better bring an army. That woman fights dirty."

LaFontaine sizes her up. "I'm just throwing this out there. She is a vampire and the possibility of her attacking us is still very much on the table. We need to get some rest before we play our next card, whatever that is. So my vote is to take precautions and leave her as is."

"That's not the worst idea you've ever had," Perry admits grudgingly.

LaFontaine says, "Let's get going." Perry tags along, leaving Carmilla and me alone.

I bring Carmilla some more blood. Call it a peace offering. "Sorry about this, but I need to get some sleep, get my strength back for tomorrow when we go after the dean. Your teeth in my neck aren't part of the plan, so the ropes stay. For now."

Carmilla settles back into her funk and I crawl into the safety of my bed.

With the covers tucked tightly around my head, I fall into a deep slumber until I hear a male voice in my room. I could have sworn I locked the door. I stay very still, not moving a muscle. I eavesdrop as he speaks to Carmilla, and I swear it sounds just like Will, Kirsch's Zeta bro. Odd, since they aren't exactly friends. She was ready to rip his spleen out, as I recall.

"Pathetic. I can't believe you let those imbeciles capture you. Mother sent me to find out if you dealt with your roommate situation." He's yelling through his teeth. I peek out from under my blanket.

My mind is reeling. Mother? What roommate situation?

"Guessing by the lump on the bed and the ropes around your arms, I take it that's a no."

"I'll take you down, Will," Carmilla threatens.

I hear him snicker. I mean, she's tied up. "I'll tell you what, I'll cut the ties off but we've got to grab your prissy little roommate and be done with her. Mother is on the warpath."

I see him cut the ropes, so I open my mouth. "Will, you need to get away from her. She's a vampire."

An evil frown spreads across his chiseled jaw as he frees her. Then he spits out something none of his frat brothers would want to hear. "She's not the only one." Will lunges for my neck! Oh God, another vampire! I dive out of his way, kicking as I fall, catching him right in the ribs. He yelps, then strikes back. Carmilla munches my cookies with her untied hands, watching us duke it out but not attempting to help at all.

"My father taught me Krav Maga," I brag.

Will takes another swing at me. "I miss the 1930s when girls didn't attack."

"So inconvenient when they fight back," Carmilla muses while chewing.

"Laugh it up all you want, kitten, Mother isn't going to be too amused that I had to finish your job since you dropped the ball," he taunts her.

"You're such a mommy's boy," she scoffs. I snort because she's getting under his skin, and Will takes another swipe to get me back.

"Careful, Hollis, I'll make you a midnight snack," he warns.

Carmilla corrects him. "Knock it off, dumbass. We don't eat targets. Plus, I'm sure you're in some hot water over the missing airhead. Do you want to be known as the guy who lost two of them?"

My mouth drops open. I'm a target.

"It might be worth it just to screw with you," he snarls at her. He leans in to nip my neck, but before his teeth can pierce my skin, Carmilla backhands him, and he flies through the air. Guess he shouldn't have untied her.

"You're going to regret that, kitty."

She takes another shot at him. "I never regret anything, little brother. You know that."

Little brother? Suddenly everything is clearer.

Will steps toward Carmilla, but just her hiss sends him packing. Next thing I know, he's halfway down the hallway, licking his wounds, and I'm alone with the other vampire. I'm rattled, to say the least, but it seems like she's on my side. I breathe a sigh of relief.

"Hey, Carm. Thanks for not letting him bite me and all. Which is really nice of you … given the fact that I —"

Before I can finish, she lunges at me, tackling me to the ground. I feel sharp incisors cutting through my skin. "Oh my

God!" I scream. She keeps sucking, holding me down. I manage to wrestle myself out from under her but I see blood dripping on my pajamas.

"You bit me!" She broke the skin. I grab the side of my neck. Blood is on my fingers. I think I'm going to faint.

"Calm down, you're not dead," Carmilla says drily. She takes one of the T-shirts on her bed and wipes my neck.

I remember every vampire movie I've ever seen, every book I've ever read. What happens after the first bite? "Oh my God, I'm a vampire," I cry.

Carmilla tries to reassure me. "It doesn't work that way, cupcake. I'm the only vampire in this relationship."

"You used me like a juice box and now I don't get an explanation?"

She flips her hair back. "I'm a vampire, Hollis. I'm out of fuel. I'm pissed off and I need my strength to stop Will from ratting me out to our mother. He's a little bitch and she will tear me limb from limb if she finds out." She starts packing her duffel bag, tossing random stuff in.

"So you're just going to run away?" I ask.

"You heard what I said about my mother, right? Hell, yes, I'm fleeing. She is the devil."

I know full well that's the end of me. My voice is very small now. "Then they'll just come after me and kill me?"

"Sorry, cutie, you really never had much of a chance anyway. Nothing personal."

I whip my head around to face her. "Bull. It's totally personal. Will, your brother — nice touch — wants to kill me just to piss you off. Right now, it's your word against his. If you run, you're automatically guilty. And I'm, like, dead." It's a long shot, but I try to appeal to her sensitive side. The other night I thought she cared …

She thinks it over. "So you're implying that my best chance is to stay here and figure out how to justify protecting you?"

"That's what I'm thinking," I admit. Fingers crossed. Carmilla stops tossing things into her bag, plops down on the bed. "I have nothing even resembling a plan. So all right. I'm in. But don't think I've forgotten the last two weeks of my captivity," she warns. "I'm still pissed."

I can't believe her nerve. "*You're* pissed? You've done nothing but lie to me *and* you bit me."

"You tied me up and not for fun."

I blush. "You still have your sense of humor, I see."

"I'm taking a shower. Feel free to join me. I won't bite. Again," she adds, cackling, trying to get a rise out of me.

Carmilla disappears into the bathroom while I have a mini meltdown. A pack of vampires wants to kidnap me, and the only thing stopping them is my not-quite-as-evil vampire roommate. So that's not too complicated. Crap, I have a women's studies midterm in three hours. If the vampires don't kill me, my father will.

I'm so dead.

• TWELVE •

That sound you heard was me bombing my women's studies midterm. Pretty sure I just failed a test for the first time in my life. I can hear my father's lecture playing on Repeat in my head. He's not going to care that my attention has been wandering. You know, due to a vampire living in my room.

I trek from the test to my room. I'll just see how many peanut butter cookies I can eat in one sitting, I decide. That'll help. "I can't believe this," I groan as I settle onto my bed.

"What are you whining about now?" my unconcerned room-mate asks.

I jump. "I didn't see you. You sure are quiet for a vampire."

"We're stealth," she says, smirking.

"I think I failed my women's studies midterm." I hate even putting those words out to the universe.

Carmilla flops down dangerously close to me. "Big deal. You're dating the TA. It's not like she's going to let you tank."

"I wouldn't call it dating," I say.

"Well, she thinks you are, so just toss it out to her."

We're nose to nose. "You mean ask her to … Oh, no way. An A is a sacred trust."

"Well, if I were your TA, you wouldn't even have to ask," she drops suggestively.

I resist the urge to reach for her because, well, she might bite me, but I really want to. "That's really considerate. Unethical but considerate."

"Are you complimenting me, cupcake?" She's making me blush.

"Maybe I am."

"It looks good on you." She takes my wrist in her soft hand. "Where's the bracelet I gave you? I thought you said you liked it."

I reach under my bed to find it. Carmilla fastens it around my wrist, lightly running her finger down my arm. What is her obsession with this thing?

"What exactly does it do?" I ask.

"It wards off unwanted guests. It gives off a scent only detectable by vampires. Like if one is stalking you and catches wind of it, they would move away from you and move on to someone else. Some chemical reaction. So they claim. Well worth it to keep you safe from unwelcome vampires. Unlike myself."

She really does have some humanity under those fangs. "That's handy. Any word from the dean or Will? Or should I call them your mother and brother?" That's so bizarre I'm not sure I can do it.

Carmilla thumbs through a magazine. "Radio silence, which isn't bad. We're still breathing. A definite plus."

That doesn't exactly calm me down, but the sight of Carm lying across the bed with the sunlight hitting her face just so … does. I'd swear she was an angel if I didn't know she was a bloodthirsty demon. Yep, I'm thinking those kinds of thoughts about a vampire.

A really beautiful, sexy vampire.

Then LaFontaine and Perry burst through the door, attached at the hip. They see Carmilla sprawled next to me on the bed and their mouths drop at the same time.

"At what point in this century did people give up on knocking?" Carmilla asks.

"It's this room," I say.

LaFontaine freaks, dancing around. "The vamp is loose, Laura. It. Is. Free. Run. Where's all the garlic?"

Perry races out the door. "I'll get help." All of this turmoil has been hardest for her. Her tidy, neat world is no longer.

"Hold up!" I yell. "Calm down. I untied her. She's on our side." They don't need to know that it was actually Will who freed her. Or that he's her brother. Or that the dean is her mother and wants me dead. That's way too much of an information dump.

LaFontaine rolls her eyes. "How do you know she didn't pod-person you? Maybe she's just spewing vampire speak?"

Carmilla clears her throat. "It doesn't work that way."

"Then maybe you should tell us just how it does work. Enlighten us, why don't you? What happens to all the girls you take?"

Carmilla gets serious. "I honestly don't know what happens once they go to my mother."

"I'm not following. Your mother?" LaFontaine asks.

Carmilla eyeballs me. "Do you want to tell them or should I?"

So much for keeping a secret. "The dean is Carmilla's mother."

That nearly knocks LaFontaine over.

"That is beyond the weird of Silas. So the dean, your mom, is a killer who is kidnapping girls."

Carm nods.

"And you've been helping her?" LaFontaine gets in her face.

I interrupt. "Her mother ... the dean, has been playing this game for the last several hundred years."

"Game?" LaFontaine asks.

"She makes Carmilla trick girls, then she drugs them or something. Carm doesn't know what happens to them after that."

LaFontaine turns to Carmilla. "So you just serve them up like pizzas?"

When she puts it that way, it does sound preposterous. Carmilla gives it right back. "Gee, Mom, wanna share the ancient secrets of your vampire cult with me? You don't? Oh, if

I keep asking, you'll tear my head off and hand it to me. Whatever it is that she does to them, their blood is undrinkable after it happens. That's all that I know."

LaFontaine thinks that over. "If it's affecting their blood chemistry, it might be physically affecting their brains."

"Makes total sense to me," says Carmilla.

"I wonder if the sludge on the notes left behind with the abductions can help us," LaFontaine says. "Maybe it's the key. I need to get to the lab and rush the results."

"Will that help us get Betty back?" I question. I still want to help her, even if my new roommate is not what she seemed at first.

Carmilla sighs. "Hollis, there is no getting her or any of them back. Have I been unclear? The only thing left to do is to stay out of my mother's way. There's no scenario in which we cross her."

I hold up my wrist, with the bracelet dangling. "But you've been saving girls."

"No. I've just been screwing with Mommy dearest and her band of minions to annoy her."

I'm stunned, completely taken aback. "After all that she did, your revenge is to be annoying? You've got to be kidding me. I thought you were a centuries-old badass."

"There's a reason I lived to be centuries old. When it comes to my mother, I pick my battles. She has a pedigree of evil unlike any other."

Carmilla must see my expression of disbelief, because now she gets up in my face. "You are no match for her. You are a teenager whose only real skill is snooping around in other people's business."

I'm so close that I feel the breeze of her breath with every word. I almost feel her heartbeat.

"But you're a world-class killer vampire. I know what you can do if you really want to."

She thinks about that, even half grins. Then she gets all flustered. "That … that has nothing to do with it. Guess what, right now, you have a better chance of taking me down than I've ever had against my mother. She is the queen of all things wicked."

Before I can answer, Perry returns with help. Danny rushes through the door wielding a stake. She dives at Carmilla. "Get away from her!" Like I need her to protect me or something.

I maneuver myself between them, holding my hand up to Danny to stop. "It isn't what it looks like, Danny! No!"

Before I can separate them, Danny and Carmilla attack each other. Or actually Carmilla swoops over Danny, dropping her in a nanosecond, holding her head on the desk. From the corner of her smothered mouth, Danny manages, "I won't let you hurt her."

"She isn't the one in trouble. I've been very patient with all your antics," Carmilla hisses at Danny, still applying pressure to her neck. "I'm trying to remember why I haven't just killed you yet."

I wedge myself between them. "Danny's sorry, aren't you?" I say. I poke her. She wiggles her head up and down, and Carmilla relents.

"I'm just trying to protect you," Danny tells me.

"I've got this," I say.

"It doesn't look like it. And I don't know why you have to post all these crazy videos that rile everyone up. It's just too much — you're playing with fire, and it's dangerous."

Perry and LaFontaine back off, and Carmilla almost seems to be enjoying our angry exchange.

"It's important that the truth come out," I tell Danny. "To be clear, I don't need a babysitter or another dad. I get that you're brave and I really like you, but we aren't exactly a couple."

Danny looks at Carmilla. "Is this because of her?"

I look at Carmilla, too. Like I can actually keep my eyes off her. "No, it's because of me. And you. Needing different things." I sound lame, I know it, but I have to be honest with Danny. I do care about her and if Carmilla wasn't in the picture, things might be different. But she is and I can't do anything about it. I don't know how it happened, but it did. I fell for a vampire.

The sadness in Danny's eyes eats at me. "Sure, Laura. I'll back off." She heads to the door with some final words for Carmilla. "If anything happens to her, I'm coming back for you with a stake."

Carmilla dismisses her. "I'll be waiting."

Danny takes my elbow. "I guess I'll see you in class."

The air is heavy, like the silence in the room. And then suddenly an ominous rumbling starts outside the window, followed by a deflating sound like a tire losing air. Carmilla runs to the window. "What the hell?"

She slams the window shut. I join her as we watch giant mushrooms exploding, sending spores blasting into the windowpanes. Terrified, I grab Carmilla's arm. In the quad, people are screaming and running aimlessly.

Perry latches on to LaFontaine, who eyeballs the spores that continue to splat against our window. They just keep coming, one after another. I can't believe this is happening. I hope the window doesn't shatter.

"This is not good," I say. Understatement of the year.

"I hate this place," mutters Carmilla.

I thought I did, too.

Until I fell for Carm.

· THIRTEEN ·

Sleeping at my desk is becoming my new normal. Today, the smell of fresh coffee rouses me. Carmilla sets a steaming hot cup of java in front of me. "Thought you could use this," she says sweetly.

"Long night."

She wipes dirt off my cheek with the edge of her T-shirt.

"The Alchemy Club lost control of this underground fungus," I mumble, still half-asleep. "It owned Twitter last night. I was Snapchatting as it all unfolded."

"Of course you were. You record everything. It's a sickness."

So not fair! "Just because you conked out once the initial mushroom blast hit us. I couldn't sleep with the campus under siege by out-of-control spores. I had to get involved. Help the cause. When I got home, I was glued to social media. I must have fallen asleep …"

"The Alchemy idiots are such boneheads," Carmilla mutters.

I agree. "Anyone breathing that crap in started lurching around like a zombie. It was like *The Walking Dead* out there."

"That part was pretty funny," she admits.

She can't be serious. I have to stop her. "Right up until the zombies tried to burn down the Lustig Theater Building. They didn't succeed."

"Still pretty damn funny."

I look at the images on my computer. "Then they attacked anyone who tried to stop them. Like a mass slaughter."

"Still …"

"You can pretend all you want. I know you aren't this insensitive. You leaped into action as soon as the first mushroom hit. Everyone saw you save me." I point at the webcam. Carmilla shifts around uncomfortably.

"I was saving myself from the spores." She isn't very convincing. I snuggle up next to her.

"Sure you were. Those of us who didn't get covered in that cloud of mushroom dust — thank you, again — spent the evening hacking apart six-foot toadstools and rolling barrels of fungicide into the basement of any building within a half-mile radius of the Lustig."

"Just another night at Silas," she jokes.

"Didn't the students try to torch the Lustig in 1904?"

"You're so cute when you nerd out over Silas history."

I blush. "It was where all of the plays were held." Now I'm showing off a little bit but she thinks it's cute.

"No one likes theater nerds. Never have."

The door swings open. Perry and LaFontaine shuffle in, both exhausted, Perry in full denial mode. "That was nutty last night, wasn't it? Probably some sorority initiation or pledge prank. My hair smells like a portobello sandwich."

Carmilla and I share a glance. LaFontaine catches us. "Don't bother. She just can't go there." Perry drops on the bed, holding her head in her hands, and I reach out to rub her back. Poor thing, she's even more traumatized than the rest of us.

"Did you see Danny?" says LaFontaine. "She was a force, very Wonder Woman. Ripping those toadstools up with her bare hands. Good thing she's still on our side in spite of the whole Hollis situation."

"I'm standing right here," I say.

Carmilla groans at the mention of Danny. She does that whenever Danny's name comes up now, holding a grudge after the wrongful tying-up fiasco. "Danny's been prone to acting out of late," Perry says. "Lots of pent-up aggression. You know."

"I think she's still mad at me," I admit.

"Yeah, I'd steer clear for a while," LaFontaine recommends.

Carmilla stands up. "Not that you aren't welcome, but why are you two here?"

Now LaFontaine is all business. "The tests came back for the sludge we found in Sarah Jane and Nat's room," they say.

"And?"

"It was cerebrospinal fluid," LaFontaine explains.

Perry emits a high-pitched whine of distress.

"Is that what I think it is?" I have to ask.

"It's the fluid in your brain," LaFontaine confirms. Yep, it's my worst nightmare.

"I touched Betty's brain fluid?" I say, hyperventilating. "I seriously think I'm going to throw up."

"And there's more …"

Carmilla smirks. "More than brain matter?"

LaFontaine starts to pace. "I ran a sample through the electron microscope, and that's when I found these." They lean over me and plug a USB key into my computer, clicking a few times while we peer over their shoulder. When the pictures come up, everyone except for LaFontaine shrieks.

There are wormlike creatures squiggling all over the screen. Perry starts to gag, and even Carmilla averts her eyes. "What the hell are those?" I yell.

"Don't look at me, I'm just a vampire," Carmilla says, cringing.

I study them even though my stomach is churning. "This could be why Betty and the others started acting so strange. Parasites will do that to you."

"Exactly!" LaFontaine exclaims. They turn to Carmilla and ask, "During your mother's game, was there something you gave the girls or made them drink that could have caused this?"

Carmilla squirms. "If that's happening to them, it's after Mother takes them. I'm not privy to that. Never was."

Is she telling us the truth? LaFontaine pushes her to say more. "Think it over. You spent hundreds of years with your … mother. Granted, you had that brief period underground. Any nugget might help."

"Not a fan of dredging up every excruciating detail of my painful past. This isn't therapy," Carmilla groans, then leaves the room. I want to follow, but we have to finish this.

LaFontaine tries to level with me. "I don't want to make her uncomfortable, but she's the one that would have the goods on her mom."

"She lost someone she cared about, so this is upsetting her," I explain. "She's feeling something human … which probably makes her want to eat nails."

LaFontaine can see right through me. "Crushing much?"

"I just feel bad for her," I say, hedging. "The way her mother treats her. She's a monster. No wonder she has so much baggage."

"That may be, but I wanna figure this out before that baggage crushes us or, worse, bites us. We know the dean has her vamp army kidnap girls, infect them with brain parasites and then kidnap them again … but why?"

Wait a second. What if there's another explanation?

"What if they don't?" I wonder.

LaFontaine is perplexed. "Not following."

"Let's break it down. Parasites have life cycles, right?" I did learn something in high school science. LaFontaine nods. I continue with my theory. "So what if the girls vanishing the second time has nothing to do with vampires?"

"I don't get it."

"What if it's just the next stage of the parasite? What if this is something we haven't seen yet?"

Perry has been quiet for a long time, but all of a sudden she's panicked. "No. No. No. I demand that you all stop this. Vampires, brain parasites, evil mushrooms. Just no. All I want is movie night and a formal dance at the end of the term. You're supposed to come to me with relationship problems. Normal college stuff. Not this. *Be normal*."

She makes a valid point.

LaFontaine goes over to her. "A little dramatic, even for you," they tease. Perry smacks her.

"I know this is all fun and games for you, Susan, but you can't expect all of us to go along with this insanity."

"It's the way it is. Weird. Like I've been saying. You can't make the world conform to your comfort level. It doesn't work that way."

Perry relents, though she isn't exactly a good sport about it. "Fine. That doesn't mean you have to throw yourself into every single bizarre situation you come across. You won't even let me call you Susan anymore."

Steam comes out of LaFontaine's ears. "I do not want to be

Susan anymore! My name isn't Susan. It's LaFontaine. As a reminder, I do not identify as male or female. I insist you treat me as such. It's quite simple: call me LaFontaine and use 'they,' 'their' or 'them' or I will not respond."

Perry holds her ground. "That's too bad. Because Susan was my friend. This LaFontaine ... I don't even know who she is anymore."

"They," I correct her.

Perry storms out, and LaFontaine is crushed. I don't know what the hell to do, so I offer some chocolate. "You okay?"

"Just peachy. My best friend since I was five thinks I'm a freak now because I no longer identify as Susan."

I put my arm around LaFontaine's shoulder. "She'll come around. Let's leave all the vampire fighting alone and watch a movie. Stuff our faces with popcorn and candy."

A moment passes. LaFontaine nods, worn out. "Sounds good. Just not *Twilight*."

•

LaFontaine and I drift into slumber after back-to-back movies. Popcorn litters the bed, along with soda cans and candy wrappers. The signs of a perfect evening. Deep into sleep, I sense the nightmare creep in. I feel myself screaming and flailing around.

Carmilla shakes me awake. "Laura. It's just a dream." I don't even remember her coming back.

I sit straight up and cling to her. "So much blood. It was filling the room. Then it was an ocean with a bright light shining over it." Carmilla holds me close and my eyes fill with tears.

LaFontaine responds, "That's not creepy. Does this mean that Hollis has been picked?"

Carmilla is still embracing me. "She shouldn't be having the dreams anymore at all. The bracelet should have chased vampires and darkness away."

LaFontaine's gaze lingers on Carmilla's arms around me. "The bracelet's not very effective. Maybe it's defective."

Not gonna lie, I'm still pretty shaken up by the dream. "It wasn't a vampire. It was a girl. Standing in all the blood. She didn't even try to swim. She just stood there," I whisper softly.

Carmilla squeezes calm into me. "Did she say anything?"

"She said I shouldn't go into the light because the light was hungry," I remember.

"I'm never going to sleep again," LaFontaine says.

"That's all she said?"

I notice that I'm entwined with Carmilla, and LaFontaine is watching. I extricate myself slowly and share a wild idea. "Sorry. Um. Yeah. The girl in the dream … it's Ell, isn't it?"

Carmilla's eyes crinkle and a teardrop falls down her cheek. "I don't know. I've never seen her. The girls we took would talk about how she looked in their dreams. They said she wore a white dress. Had a mole on her left cheek. She's never reached out directly to me, though …" Sorrow covers her face like a shadow.

"I'm confused. Who is Ell?" says LaFontaine.

"Carm's ex. Sort of. She got taken by the dean a long, long time ago."

"The light is hungry? Not to go all peculiar facts again, but this might be a legit clue. It might have something to do with the parasite?" LaFontaine throws out.

I think about that for a moment. "Could be. But how are we going to cross-reference some ancient evil light and brain worms?"

LaFontaine picks up her phone. "I'll google worms and evil light."

"Oh, that'll help," Carmilla says sarcastically. "Not. You need the archives in the library, from around the time when my mother first came here in the 1800s. I remember there was some guy who'd done research that could have exposed her."

"What happened to him?" I ask.

"He ... disappeared."

You could hear a pin drop.

"Do you know where the archives are in the library? We'll just pop over there."

Carmilla scoffs. "I'll have to show you. You don't just pop over. They're housed in a subbasement that exists only after dark."

Naturally, here at Silas our archives come and go as they please.

"We need to protect ourselves when we go," I say. We're not

taking any chances, what with mushrooms and vampires on the prowl.

Carmilla watches as we gather up headlamps and faux weapons — a flat iron, a jar of pennies and Betty's Buddha desk statue — to prepare for our fact-finding mission. She rolls her eyes. "How did you all ever trap me? Not my most shining moment."

I turn on the webcam and speak directly into it. My audience needs to know what's coming next. I say in a low voice, "Though it's risky, we have to go to the library after dark to find the research we need to uncover the mystery of the disappearing students of Silas. We have no choice."

"Yeah," LaFontaine echoes rather enthusiastically. "We will not be denied!"

I explain, "If we don't come back, Danny, Perry, we're sorry we didn't listen to you."

LaFontaine grabs my shoulder. "Oh, hell no. No apologies. We embrace the weird. Bring it. We are making weird our bitch!" The words are screamed into the webcam just before the video is posted. Carmilla and I exchange a glance.

The three of us head to the library, hiding behind trees and dodging other students, all in an effort to remain undercover.

"There's a window in the back of the library that has a broken lock. It hasn't worked since 1810," Carmilla whispers. "We can climb in, and no one will see us."

I had no idea vampires could be so useful.

We make it inside the library with no problem, and our

flashlights show the way as we hurry to the subbasement. Every step we take brings a sense of foreboding.

"Did you feel that cold breeze?" I ask.

Neither of them answers. Carmilla just shushes me.

Carm opens a door and guides us through it. It slams shut, scaring the crap out of me. LaFontaine grabs my arm. If Carm is freaked out, she's hiding it well.

We climb down the stairs, slip through dark aisles and eventually come to an area that looks like a cave. Carmilla stops. "This is it," she says.

The temperature drops at least twenty degrees and lights start to flash all around us. I see a wall of old-school computer screens, and a man starts talking to us when LaFontaine turns one on. Yes, he's inside the computer. Because this is Silas and nothing is normal.

"Hello, I'm J. P. I work here," he says. "Can I help you?"

Carmilla is unfazed and gets in front of the screen. "Do you know anything about students going missing? A hungry light? Brain-eating parasites?"

My breathing is fast and ragged. I am seriously scared. Where is the dean right now? Can she see us? Will we be next?

"You look just like your mother," J. P. says. Lightning strikes and we all jump.

"Let's get out of here!" I scream.

"No way. We've come this far," says LaFontaine. "We have to know!"

J. P. whispers, "All the information is right here in my research. Take the big book."

The big book? I grab the largest one I see — it must weigh ten pounds — and step away. We've got what we need — we have to go!

LaFontaine pops a USB key into the port on the side of the gigantic hard drive of the computer. J. P. disappears, then a download starts.

Footsteps echo in my ears. Someone's coming. We hear screams, then a series of explosions. This is it.

"Run!" Carmilla yells.

The computer screen blows up as soon as LaFontaine removes the USB key. Smoke chases us up the stairs, and for some reason we are hit with flying goop as we flee. I can't wait to take a shower. But we manage to run all the way back to the dorm.

•

The memory of tonight's activities will be engraved on my brain forever. In terms of nightmarish and insane, this was legend. Even the shower and scrubdown didn't help. While Carmilla chugs blood straight from the bag, LaFontaine continues a dogged pursuit of all the weird, popping the USB key into my computer. I sit in front of the camera to update the student body.

"We survived the research trip. Which we will never speak of again. Ever."

Carmilla and LaFontaine nod, finally agreeing on something. I raise the gargantuan book above my head. "Here's our haul. One gnarly Sumerian book circa before time began."

LaFontaine types furiously on the keyboard. "Check it out. The rescued digital consciousness of J. P. Armitage, the junior records clerk and Silas student. Class of 1874. Meet the internet, J. P." A hologram of one J. P. Armitage pops up. He looks so distinguished with his longish hair, glasses with round frames and plaid bow tie.

I do the play-by-play for my audience. "Because someone really did get absorbed into the library catalog. The folklore is true. Though how he got sucked in a hundred years before anything was digitized is iffy ..." I explain.

J. P. waves frantically. "He's kinda cute," LaFontaine whispers to me. I soldier on.

"Per J. P.'s research, there was a rash of disappearances back in 1874. He didn't have an electron microscope to test his theory about brain parasites, but he did dig up information on the hungry light and a vampire contingent serving it."

Carmilla speaks up. "Let me guess. My mother was leading the pack."

"Yep. She and her special council. Once J. P. got close to the truth, though, he became absorbed."

"Well," Carmilla chimes in, "übernerd better have more

than 'hungry' and 'eats girls.' We need more information than that. This entire book is filled with that kind of stuff."

"What do you mean?" I question her.

Carmilla flips the book open and starts to read to us. "'Yogoth, raised with twelve virgins burned at the stake; Kalos, the sprinkled blood of virgins on the roots of the sacrificial tree; Nyarlothog, Spinner of Lies, prefers the livers of virgins force-fed red wine for three days.'"

I shake my head. "Not very subtle. Who are these guys?"

"No idea. Maybe ancient vampires," she cracks.

A light tap on the door interrupts us. Perry pokes her head in, surveys the room. "Oh, good, you're all here. I had to check on you. Because, you know, I saw the last video. I needed to make sure you weren't dead."

She tries to make eye contact with LaFontaine, who avoids her like the plague. They've been on the serious outs since the big fight, and LaFontaine is clearly not in the mood for this now. Perry huffs and leaves again, almost as fast as she arrived.

I reach out and pat LaFontaine on the shoulder. "She'll come around. You're awesome, and this stuff is just tough for her to wrap her brain around. We'd be nowhere without you."

LaFontaine hugs me and then turns back to the hologram. "J. P., let's you and me hit my anatomy book and see what we can figure out about how these pesky parasites work."

J. P. responds with a thumbs-up. LaFontaine pops the USB

key out and J. P. disappears. LaFontaine salutes us on their way out the door.

Carmilla and I are finally alone. The lamp's amber tone gives her face a beautiful glow. Her cheekbones are so high, like a model's. Her glowing face is so inviting.

And her lips ...

I'm not sure who turned up the heat, but I feel sweat beads on the back of my neck. It's so quiet that I can almost hear myself think. Carmilla's eyes are melting me. I break the quiet and say, "Hey, thanks for coming with us to the library. We needed you. I needed you."

She half smiles. "I like that."

I reach for her. "You went because you want to know what happened to Ell. Don't you? Because you're hoping you can save her somehow?" I feel a twinge of jealousy, but you can't be jealous of a dead person. Can you?

She doesn't look up, and her voice breaks. "Ell is dead. That I know. And my mother is responsible."

"Still."

"Don't start expecting heroic vampire bullshit from me, cupcake. I know better than to tangle with my mother."

"So," I tease, "if you don't want me getting heroic notions about you, you should probably stop saving my life."

She can't help mellowing and crawls close to me. "If you were gone, who would buy the cookies?" We fall back on her bed and continue to read in silence. Side by side. Shoulders nuzzled. A world of questions hanging between us. She makes the cutest sound when she's breathing.

I roll over, opening my eyes and squinting when the sun hits them. Wait, that means I slept through the night for the first time since I got to Silas. Apparently on Carmilla's shoulder. "Nothing like a good night's sleep," I announce. "Hey, sleepyhead," I say, nudging Carm. She's like a brick. "I dreamt about that damn cat again but it was curled up on my rug, napping."

Carm grunts, pulls her pillow over her face.

In the past, the cat in my dream was scary, like it was going to attack me or even kill me. Not last night, though. Everything means something, but I think this is just a cat.

"I have to study this morning. I haven't been to class in two weeks. I'm so behind," I tell her.

Carm hits me with a pillow. "Shhhhhhh. Sleeping."

Perry bursts in, a total wreck. Hair flat, clothes wrinkled. Is that coffee on her sleeve? She races around the room, searching for something. "Where is she?" she demands. I have no clue what she's talking about.

She launches into an explanation. "I know things have been tense with us, but her hiding out is ridiculous. Just tell me where she is."

Ah. That. "It's 'they,' not 'she,' and I don't know. LaFontaine isn't here, Perry."

"No, she ... they ... have to be. This has to be some kind of a joke. But I'm not laughing. Because it's not funny."

I'm lost.

She babbles nervously. "LaFontaine's side of the room is a mess, and this was stapled to the door."

I take it from her and read it out loud. "'Your nosy little friend no longer attends Silas University because (a) she meddled in things that were none of her business, (b) did you really think we wouldn't find out what you were up to? (c) we are ancient and terrible and (d) none of you are safe. Exit procedures have already commenced. No action on your part is required.'"

Carmilla shoots up. "Shit."

Perry is freaking out, pacing in circles. She might just wear a hole in the floor. "It's the vampires. They could have taken them anywhere. They could be doing anything to them. Awful things. We have to find them before it's too late." Her voice rises with fear.

Carm attempts to calm her. "My money is on LaFontaine being with the others who are missing. They're down by two and need bodies."

"What are you saying?" Perry asks.

"My mother and her posse. They need five girls for the ritual. They have Betty, Natalie and Elsie. They lost Sarah Jane, you know, since they killed her, and I've kept them from taking Laura, so they need two more people," Carm explains. She points at my bracelet.

Oh God. Now I see what that was all about. Unfortunately, Perry does, too.

Perry flips out. Like, I never knew she could be so loud. "So because you protected Laura, they took LaFontaine!" she shouts. "Why didn't you give them a bracelet? How could you not protect them?"

I just stare at Carmilla, waiting for the answer.

"No matter who I help, my mother's group always takes more. It's just the way it is. I had no idea it would be your friends. I told you I wasn't a hero, cupcake." An unmistakable melancholy fills her voice.

Perry isn't finished. She turns and blasts me next. "You did all of this! Alerting the would-be kidnappers at every turn. They know your every move, thanks to that vlog. I hope you're happy. What if they're implanting parasites in LaFontaine's brain? What if the last thing they remember is that I was awful to them? I want to take it all back," she whimpers. Tears pour down her face, and I help her to the bed, where she curls up in a ball.

I turn to Carmilla. "Is this all my fault? Did they take LaFontaine because you protected me? Did they really see the videos?"

Carmilla has no patience for this. "This is a bad look, cupcake. Don't be so naive. Unless *you* kidnapped a bunch of girls for some unthinkable evil, nothing that's happening here is your fault."

"Really?" I am ridiculously relieved.

Carmilla points to herself. "Former minion of evil here. Yeah, you're good. This is on my mom. All of it."

I sniffle. "We have to warn anybody who might be in harm's way. They still need someone else." I step toward the computer, but Carmilla grabs my arm.

"Why must you continue to do this? Just say no to the webcam. My mother must be ripping her hair out in clumps she's so pissed. Which is the only good thing about the videos."

I speak directly to the webcam. "Silas students, you are all in danger. All of you." I know I sound unhinged but people are dropping like flies. (And I like to have the last word.)

"Laura, quick question before you implode," says Carmilla. "Did you happen to tell that big puppy who follows you around that his BFF is a vampire?" Will, her brother.

My eyes bug out. "Oh my God, Kirsch." I fly out the door, Carmilla at my heels. We race across campus and find Kirsch in the quad playing Ultimate Frisbee. When he sees us, he flexes his muscles.

"Does that work?" Carmilla asks. Her arms are crossed as she sizes him up.

"Not on me," I say.

Kirsch swaggers over. "Did you hotties come to watch me destroy the Sigs on the Frisbee field?"

I just cannot with the "hottie" right now. Carmilla cocks her arm back like she's going to clock him, and I barely stop her by grabbing her elbow. "We need to talk to you."

"You changed your mind and want to date me?"

"She didn't lose her grip on reality," Carmilla cracks.

Kirsch looks hurt. "You're mean," he says.

"This isn't about who I want to date. It's about Will."

"My main bro."

Frisbees whiz by and Kirsch cranes his neck to watch.

I wish I could soften the blow, but there's no easy way to say this, so I just blurt it out. "Your main bro is a vampire."

Kirsch takes a step back like he's been punched in the gut and throws his arms out. His jaw drops open. "No way. Why are you lying to me? I've always been so nice to you." He glances at Carmilla. "Even to her. Mostly. Will is my guy. And he was your dudescort."

His heart is breaking, but I can't mince words. I rest my hand on his shoulder. "Sorry, Kirsch, it's the truth. Will is a full-blown vampire. He snuck into my room to kidnap me like he did the others. He practically admitted it. Carmilla saved me."

"Dude. Just no. He came with me to Sarah Jane's memorial. Who would do that?"

"A vampire," Carmilla answers. "Vampires can be very shady and sneaky. Trust me, I know."

He's so still that he could be hypnotized.

"I'm really sorry, Kirsch."

He's lost in his own world. "The memorial is so nice. A little rock with her name on it. I've been visiting it every day. Bringing pink flowers. Pink was her favorite color."

"I know this must be difficult for you to understand," I sympathize.

Poor guy. He tilts his head to me. "I get that you want to help me out because you think I'm dumb. I might not know a lot about math or science but I do know bros. We would walk through fire for each other. That includes Will. He might be a vampire but he's a Zeta bro first."

He's convincing, but Carmilla cuts him off. "That isn't the way it works, stud."

"Well, he's never tried to bite me," he argues.

"He almost killed me," I counter.

That's when Kirsch completely changes the subject. "Maybe you should take a break from fighting evil. The Zetas are having an end-of-term party on Friday. We're wrapping the goat in bacon this year. Gotta get back to it." He waves as he heads out to play Frisbee, not a care in the world.

Carmilla shakes her head. We tried, the flash in her eyes says. "You can send a dude to college but you can't make him think," she cracks.

•

When we get back to the dorm, Carmilla locks the door right away. "We have got to curb the traffic in here."

I like where her head is at. No interruptions. For once.

She places her hand on the small of my back. "You okay?"

"I was thinking about Kirsch and his brothers. It might be nice not to have anything to worry about except going to parties. That must sound silly to you. With all the grand parties you've been to all over the world."

"Yeah, but for most of them I was bait in a vicious supernatural game. That takes the fun out of it. You know?"

"Good point. What did kids do for fun back then?" I ask.

"Same as now. Got drunk. Danced our asses off. The booze wasn't as refined. There wasn't any flavored vodka. Waltzing was practically forbidden."

"Hold up. Waltzing was scandalous? How can that be?"

Carmilla takes my hand and tugs me up, into a waltzing pose. I smell the chocolate cookie on her breath. Her eyes meet mine.

"Partners face to face, chest to chest. Not a piece of paper between them." She whirls me around. "Spinning round and round the dance floor. So close. In 1698, it might as well have been sex."

My head is still spinning, though we have ceased whirling around the room. The butterflies in my belly are on high alert. She is sexy. This is sexy.

I'm all in.

· FOURTEEN ·

Sitting on the steps of the library, I call my dad. It's the time of the week where I check in, and my dorm is too chaotic for this talk. It's quiet here, plus I can bend the truth without anyone commenting.

"Hi, Dad, how's it going?"

He's having the family room redone. That's nice. I'm battling vampires and he's picking out sofas.

"Yep, classes are great. I just left the library. I've been there all day."

I listen. He's proud of me. Great.

"No, I'm not going out, I'm studying tonight. Just going to pick up a salad or something healthy for dinner." I nod as he describes the dimensions of his new TV. "Yeah. Love you, too."

I lied. I've never lied to my father before, unless you count the time that I filled his vodka bottle with water after my friends and I raided the liquor cabinet when he went away for the weekend. I blamed it on my uncle Lester.

In my defense, lying was the only option. Explaining that I haven't had much time to study, given the fact that I've been dodging death and hunting for missing students, would land me in a heap of trouble. I'm committed to an all-nighter that doesn't involve investigating anything.

On the way back to my dorm, I stop for provisions at the campus market, psyching myself up for all things English lit and American history. A six-pack of orange soda, cookies, candy, beef jerky and a family-size bag of chips. I skip the dip. That would be gluttonous.

I pass Perry in the hall on her hands and knees scrubbing the baseboards, and I manage to get by without her noticing. For some reason she's fixated on a spot in the corner. I feel bad trying to avoid her but she's been guilting me every chance she gets about LaFontaine, and tonight I just need a break.

Opening my door, I'm greeted by multicolored twinkle lights and soft music. The room has been transformed. Carmilla steps out from behind the door in leather and lace, holding a bottle of champagne. She throws her hand out. "Welcome to Chez Vampire. Anyone can meet you at a cheesy restaurant." That makes me warm all over. She's got the table set with candles and votives lighting up our room. It's beautiful.

Like her.

"Wow!" is all I've got.

"You like?"

"You're very romantic — for a vampire."

She grins. "Years of practice."

She takes the six-pack of orange soda, setting it on the nightstand. She replaces it with a glass of bubbly. She raises her glass to mine. "To an evening without interruption or that webcam."

I raise my glass and gently clink hers. "Something smells amazing. Did you cook?"

She slides a chair out for me to sit down. I remind myself that she's a vampire and may be setting me up. The way I did to her. She places a plate of pasta with sauce and meatballs in front of me. "Family recipe that dates back to the 1800s."

"How many times have you made this?" What I really mean is how many girls have been seduced with this very same meal. I mean, she's been around for a long time.

"Once. Today."

Vampire or not, she's getting under my skin. In a good way. Silas surprises me at every turn. When I arrived, love never even entered my mind, and now it's right in front of me.

Carmilla settles in across from me with those come-on eyes. "Taste it."

I twirl my fork in the pasta, making sure to cover it in sauce. It tastes like Italy. "Mmmm. This is the best pasta I've ever eaten. The sauce is phenomenal!" I lose a strand or two on my chin.

"My turn," she says, using her thumb to wipe away the

red droplets. "Wait till you bite into a meatball. My great-grandmother was known for them. It's how she lured my great-grandfather in."

I chomp down one of these balls of amazing. "Is that what you're doing to me?"

"Only if it's working."

I drop my fork and go to her, moving her chair back.

She takes my hand in hers and asks, "Waltz?"

Her arms go around me and she pulls me close. I let her.

She has her answer.

· FIFTEEN ·

I'm not going to lie. Last night was pretty spectacular. Like on a scale of one to ten, it was a twenty. I've never before felt the feelings that are consuming me. I'm willing to overlook the whole vampire hiccup for the sunshine warming my heart.

My phone dings. Another text. I ignore it like I have all the others. It's Perry. Again.

"Do you want coffee?" I ask. I pop in a pod for me. Sumatra, extra bold this morning. A look at my phone tells me that it's actually afternoon. We stayed up all night watching a marathon of *Doctor Who* on my laptop. I had to explain everything to her. I didn't mind one bit.

"Just you," Carmilla purrs. That makes me blush.

Perry texts so many times that the dinging finally gets to Carmilla. "What does she want now?"

I read the texts aloud. "She doesn't like being in their room alone. She claims she 'sees' LaFontaine everywhere and feels their spirit."

"She's coming unglued. You know that, right?"

"That may be, but I'm responsible for it," I reply.

There's a deep sigh from the other side of the room. "Not this again."

I cross the room to her, get an inch away from her face. "You're tense." I move behind her and massage her shoulders. I lean close to her neck, barely touching her with my lips. Not everyone is a biter.

"Not that I don't love this, but what do you want?"

I feign being hurt. "Can't I just be nice to you?"

"Anytime, but my spidey sense assures me that there's more going on here. It's written all over your beautiful, guilty face."

"Okay, fine. I think we should invite Perry to hang out here with us. She's terrified that she's next on the list and that we'll never find LaFontaine."

"Just put a stake in me now."

"You have to admit that your mother has been noticeably silent."

"That's never a good sign. It means she's plotting."

What does that mean? We should all be petrified, like Perry?

She adds, "The thing about my mother is that she can be vindictive. She's spent her lifetime being a powerful player in a dark community. Will is her little puppet and he'll do anything she tells him to do. I was the only one to defy her and she buried me alive."

"So she isn't just going away?" I ask, even though I know the answer.

"Not in a million years."

Picking up my phone, I send a short text to Perry. *Why don't you come hang out here with us later?*

I take Carm's hand and bring it up to my cheek. Before I can even kiss her hand, there's a knock at the door. "That didn't take long," I joke.

"Was it even thirty seconds?" Carm sighs.

When I open the door, Perry is lugging a mop, cleaning supplies and some pots and pans.

•

I knew Perry was obsessed with all things cleaning and all things vampire. What I didn't know was that Perry never sleeps. Never. She must be chugging caffeinated energy drinks by the case.

I hear her shuffling around the room while Carmilla and I try to sleep. I toss and turn. I try to block out the noise. And finally I start to watch her.

At first she's dusting, tidying, folding the laundry. I pull the pillow over my head when I see her turn on the webcam, but I'm curious now. I keep one eye open.

"Hello, Laura's viewers," Perry whispers. "If you've been

following along, you know my best friend has been kidnapped and is still missing. I've been busy not panicking. I cleaned every surface in this filthy room. It should be noted that it's no longer a pigpen. I am not panicking."

She's totally panicking. I don't even care that she's posting on my vlog. I just need some sleep. I'm jarred awake by what you imagine would be the scent of heaven. I roll away from the wall to see Perry sitting on the edge of my bed with a plate of fresh brownies.

"Brownie? They're warm."

It's only 5:00 A.M., but it is a brownie. I hoist myself up, taking a bite of chocolaty goodness. Carmilla is asleep on the floor. She must've rolled off the bed in the middle of the night. She does that.

"We need to talk," Perry starts.

I roll closer, so groggy. "Um, okay. I'm half-asleep. It's early. I didn't sleep so well. I kept dreaming about the big black cat sleeping on the floor."

"It's just Carmilla," Perry says, pointing to the floor, waking her up by mistake. "Do you want a brownie?" she asks.

"Get that away from me," Carmilla snaps. "Be warned, once I've had my coffee, I'm going to eviscerate you."

Perry is unfazed. "Now that you're both up, it's time to formulate a plan."

Carmilla looks daggers at her. "So I woke up in hell?"

"Excuse me. LaFontaine is still missing and we need to take

action. We need to put this camera on a delay when we update the students, just in case the kidnappers are watching. No more tipping them off."

That seems reasonable. "Okay. Easy enough."

"Maybe call the police?" she continues. "Mercenaries? Bloodthirsty killers for hire?"

I need to calm her down. "Perry, we did that with Betty. The cops won't come unless they get a call from campus security. And campus security goes through the dean, so they're useless. They're all Team Dean."

Carmilla adds, "I don't have a directory for killers at large."

I see how bummed Perry seems. "I noticed some mold in the bathroom," I say. At least that perks her up. She grabs a sponge, a bucket and some cleanser. You could eat off our floors right now, but her nonstop nervous cleaning is driving me insane. Carmilla wasn't kidding — she's ready to sacrifice her at any moment.

"Can we make a break for it?" Carmilla asks.

"Nope. Time to go back to the book. Perry is traumatized but she isn't wrong. We have to make a move."

Once again, I turn to the big Sumerian book that J. P. assured us holds the answers we need to stop the dean and get our friends back. Could we have missed something?

I toss it next to Carmilla, then inch close to her. Sitting on my bed, we scour the book for clues, while Perry circles with rubber gloves and a spray bottle of Lysol. Perry is so aggressive with her sponge that she accidentally bumps Carmilla while she's chugging blood from her coffee mug. Suddenly there's blood splashed all over the page.

"Goddammit, Perry! Watch it!" Carmilla yells. She's dangerously close to her breaking point, and I don't want to know what happens next.

Perry freaks out. "I'm so sorry."

But maybe there's nothing to be sorry about at all.

Carmilla and I stare at the book, speechless. As the blood spreads, words emerge on the ancient pages. They become visible one after another as the blood spreads.

I elbow Carmilla. "Are those new words appearing because of the blood spill?"

She nods. "Of course that's happening."

Perry is basically paralyzed.

Carmilla starts to read the new passage. "It's an entry for something called Lophilformes. The light that devours. Wait, this says it's the light that demands the sacrifice of five virgins every twenty years. Maybe that's what my mother did with the girls I lured. Maybe she's feeding the light? Once the victims are marked, their world and I quote, 'narrows to celebration.'"

I nod. "Wait a second. So the light likes party girls? Does it say how to stop the sacrifice from happening?"

Carmilla keeps scanning the book. "'Old as oceans' depths ... the light that betrays all ...' blah, blah ... 'draws the devoured to it and consumes their minds, which increases the light and draws in more of the devoured.'" Those last words were tough for her to get out.

"So if it absorbs their minds, is the energy from that drawing people in?" I ask.

"That would make sense."

"And if Ell is reaching out to us, that means —"

Carmilla finishes my sentence. "They're conscious in there. They're alive."

That means Betty could still be alive. Yes!

"So the book says that every twenty years five virgins must be sacrificed to this hungry light?" Perry is still wrapping her mind around it all.

When Carmilla spells it out, it sounds outlandish. "The Sumerian says just that," she confirms.

I'm trying to imagine how to comfort Perry when suddenly a voice shouts, "Word!" and there's a figure in front of us. Right here in the flesh is LaFontaine, rocking a Violent Femmes T-shirt. We all scream.

"Why is everyone all worked up?" LaFontaine asks.

Perry rushes over. "Thank God you're back. In one piece." Perry runs her hand up and down LaFontaine's arm just to be sure she isn't seeing things.

LaFontaine looks at her blankly. "Back? Did I go somewhere?"

They kidnapped LaFontaine just like the others. The parasites in the brain erased the memory of it. Any calm we were feeling has left the building.

"No memory of it, LaFontaine?" I probe.

"I remember being here. Talking to all of you. Now I'm still here."

"You were gone for more than a day, over twenty-four hours," Perry says. "Vanished."

LaFontaine hesitates. "They took me? Are those parasites in my brain?"

The three of us do nothing to assuage the despair. We are just as miserable and uncertain, but relieved by the fact that LaFontaine is standing right in front of us.

"What do we know?" LaFontaine asks, then spots the pan of half-eaten brownies. "Please tell me you haven't wasted all day baking."

I hoist up the book. "No, with J. P.'s help we found out what's been happening. It's bigger than vampires. It's this devouring light thing called Lophil-something ..."

"Lophilformes," Carmilla says to help me out. I'm ancient-Sumerian challenged, and I don't care if she corrects me. "Basically, the dean sacrifices five girls to this mysterious light every twenty years. To find the light, we need to find the dean."

"Here I thought Silas was at the forefront of policies on feminism. Why would the dean — who is a woman — want to do something like that?" LaFontaine asks.

"Why does anyone start a cult? Wealth, power, eternal youth," Carmilla reasons.

We all snicker at that. "Is there anything in the book that

might help us get closer to some answers that would save everyone?" LaFontaine inquires.

"I think we're in Hail Mary mode," Carmilla answers.

"Well, we need something. Now!" I say.

"I get it. It's just not in this book, Laura."

Perry steps up. "Forget the book. Maybe the parasites don't like aspirin. Or cough medicine. Something we have on hand. Nasal spray — that might clear out your brain passages. Right?" Perry offers. That's a stretch but I keep quiet.

Perry comes back from the bathroom armed with everything from the medicine cabinet. "You said Hail Mary."

I watch her spray LaFontaine with nasal spray. Like all over. The mist is enveloping. "Thanks, Per," says LaFontaine.

Perry holds up Band-Aids and tampons, tossing them both to the side.

"Is it hot in here?" LaFontaine starts to peel off the T-shirt, revealing a small recording device.

I'm stunned. "Why are you wearing that?"

"Just in case" is said so matter-of-factly that it sounds plausible to the rest of us. Strap a recorder on. You never know when it might come in handy.

"Did you record your own kidnapping?"

LaFontaine shrugs. "I don't know. Maybe."

This is the break we need.

"Yes!" I yell.

Carmilla stares in disbelief. "Incompetent jackasses." That

was rude, and she notices. "Not you, my mother's minions. Who doesn't frisk a hostage? Well done, LaFontaine. Total badass."

LaFontaine shines, pleased with the compliment. Who doesn't want a high five and validation from a vampire?

We fumble with the device until we hear LaFontaine's recorded voice. "I didn't see anything when they took me, but now I'm in a small room that smells like damp limestone. Like a cave."

I can't think of anywhere on campus that has underground space other than the library, and we've been there. No water, no limestone.

There's some static in the recording before we hear many voices drift past, and then a familiar voice from another room. "I don't know what she's bitching about. We're fine. The third one went so fast we didn't have to collect her again. This one replaces the airhead, so we just need to score one more for the ritual before the new moon. Piece of cake. Crap, this one fainted."

"That's Will," Carmilla tells us. "My brother."

Perry and LaFontaine's mouths drop open. Perry manages to speak first. "Zeta Will is your brother?"

"Long story," I say.

"Vampire?" LaFontaine asks.

I nod.

The sound of a door being kicked fills the room.

Will's voice again, this time talking to LaFontaine. "Good news, wise guy. The dean will see you now."

LaFontaine's voice is barely audible. "That's okay. I know how busy she is."

There's a loud shriek, then the sound of a scuffle. There's a thump, and then the feed cuts off.

"I must have bumped it," LaFontaine says. "I'm so sorry …"

I jump in. "This is amazing! You did great. We know there are three girls alive down there. Will confirmed it."

Carmilla is not quite as comforting. "But we don't have a clue as to where they are or how to deal with my lunatic mother, let alone some ancient evil light. We're screwed."

Perry stares her down. "Don't be so negative, Carmilla."

We're not completely in the dark, as I remind my friends. "But we know there's a ritual, so maybe we just have to keep them from getting another girl before the new moon thing that Will was talking about. We just have to hang on until Friday … which is also when my lit paper is due."

"If we all get sucked into an evil underground light, no one will give a crap about your paper. There's that," Carmilla says.

LaFontaine is sitting calmly, munching on a brownie.

"You're taking this well," I note.

"I know I should be terrified but it really doesn't seem to matter much. Maybe that's a sign that they've already invaded what used to be me and my brain."

"No," Perry says anxiously, "you can't be going this fast — the others didn't go this fast."

"Maybe it's because the ritual is so close. That might be

amping up parasites. Stimulating them somehow," LaFontaine says, suddenly leaping up and dashing around the room in agitation.

"I'll keep an eye on my best friend," Perry offers, grabbing LaFontaine's hand. "Come on, let's go find some place to dance."

The two of them bop out into the hallway, leaving us to work against the clock. We have to find the cave before the deadline arrives ... or passes.

· SIXTEEN ·

After a full day of reading, Carmilla is still going strong, stretched across her bed poring through books and papers. If we can figure out where the girls are, we have a shot.

J. P.'s search window is open and running. Carm has befriended LaFontaine's buddy from the library and they're studying mystical weapons on campus. J. P. is loaded with good information.

Me, I'm tidying up the mess Carm has made. Not that this mess will matter if we're all dead. Her blood-encrusted glass makes me gag, I have to admit. She's been going through pints of that every few hours. Blood for her, coffee for me.

I'm really starting to miss having Perry and her mop around.

"Hey, bloodsucker," I joke, "help me out?" I need someone to get the bracelet back on my wrist. I'm pretty much wearing it all the time now.

"Funny." She fastens the bracelet, then slightly cocks her head and grins. "Gotta keep you safe."

Danny peeks in. It's been a while since I've seen her. She holds her gaze on Carmilla and says, "Perry said you wanted to talk to me?"

There's a lot of awkward hanging in the room.

"You look good," I blurt out.

Danny points at the webcam. "I can't believe you're still filming after what happened to LaFontaine." She's still blaming me and my posts for everything. I am not the enemy.

"Are you still watching?" I ask.

"I stopped after the library incident. It's too hard for me."

"How did you know about LaFontaine if you didn't tune in to the vlog?"

She moves from foot to foot, all edgy. "Perry filled me in on the details. Sounds like it's been all-consuming."

Now I'm the one who's anxious. "Yeah, I've been super stressed."

"I haven't seen you in class — you've missed a lot," she says.

"I've got a lot of other stuff going on." To say the least.

"You are here for school," she jokes, but that jab hits to close to home. What is she, my dad? If it wasn't already over between us, it would be now.

I fake a laugh, uncomfortable as hell. A glance from Carmilla encourages me. She knows what I need here. "About that school thing. I've been preoccupied, as you know."

She nods. "Okay." She's not going to make this easy for me.

"Can I get an extension on my paper? Just a week or so. Until after the soul-sucking ritual thing is over?" I ask.

Silence.

I lower my demands. "Three days?"

Danny's voice rises an octave. "Oh my God. I thought … How dumb am I? You wanted me to come over here because you can't stay on top of your homework?"

Carmilla is still watching.

I forge ahead. "Seriously? Trying to save four people isn't worth a few extra days to get my paper done? What did you think?"

"Nothing."

Oh crap. "Did you think I wanted to get back together?"

Carmilla perks up.

"Not anymore. I can't believe your nerve."

"My nerve? I can't believe you're being so vindictive and petty."

Danny gets right up in my face. "Easy for you to say. You didn't get dumped for a bloodsucking vampire."

"So hostile," Carmilla comments.

"This conversation is officially over," Danny says sharply. "If you're too busy with her to get your assignments done, that's your problem, not mine."

She turns toward the door. Carmilla can't resist sending her off with, "Come back never."

Danny looks back at me and snaps, "Delete my contact info from your phone."

"I guess that was a no," I say after the door slams. "She hates me. I don't blame her."

"Sore loser," Carmilla says.

"I hope you're having better luck finding us a secret weapon than I did scoring a decent grade."

Carmilla flips the pages. "Not so much. According to the great book, we've got Ascalon, an enchanted spear that kills dragons but only if you're a Christian saint. So that's out. The Holy Hand Grenade of Antioch, perfect for an influx of monstrous rabbits. For us, all zeroes."

She heaves the book against the wall. J. P.'s search engine keeps running on the computer until a query string for Blade of Hastur pops up. That gets my attention. "What about this one? The Blade of Hastur forged from Euuch, the burnt bones of star spawn, and meant to shatter all that opposes it? Sounds promising." I keep reading. "Crap. It won't work for us."

"Why not?"

I read ahead. "It's sealed in the face of a cliff in a cavern a thousand feet below sea level on the outskirts of town. Nobody could survive that, which is probably why it's there. Too dangerous to try to retrieve. How about a big bad bazooka? Obvious choice, but can it stop your mother?"

Carm perks up. "I could get it. It's not far from here."

"What? The bazooka?"

"The sword. Pressure at that depth isn't really an issue for us vampires. Vampire bonus points."

I try not to get too excited about this revelation. "But you'd be risking your life if your mother found out —"

She stops me. "My mother robbed me of the only person I ever cared about. Maybe I don't feel like letting her do that to me again." The sound of her voice as she admits that makes my heart skip a beat.

"I know you're not doing this just because of me?" I'm fishing.

"Please. Don't be ridiculous. Of course I am." She leans in to kiss me until she sees my new necklace. "Where did *that* thing come from?" she asks.

"It was on my dresser. I thought it was another present ..."

"Take it off!" she shouts. She reaches for the necklace, but when it touches her skin, she yelps like she's been scorched or stung. I try to rip it from my neck but it starts to choke me. I panic when I can't breathe. Everything goes black. I hear Carmilla whisper, "Mother?" right before I lose consciousness.

My head is muddled when I wake up. "Carmilla? What happened?"

"It's okay. The necklace was poisoned. A trap from my mother."

Whoa. "She fights dirty. Won't she be surprised when you

show up all badass with the one thing that will end her domination of Silas University. She's going down."

Carm turns slightly away from me. "Yeah. Not so sure she'll be expecting that."

Something in her demeanor isn't right. Maybe it's just the poison clouding my brain. Still, Carmilla is acting strange.

• SEVENTEEN •

The constant hammering outside of our dorm is driving me insane. They're building a huge stage for the end-of-term party out there, and when you add a blaring soundtrack of intermittent dance music, you've got a recipe for a pounding migraine and less studying than ever.

Then there's the grating sound of scraping wood, because Perry is whittling stakes like a beaver building a dam. You know, because vampires.

Carmilla is loosening LaFontaine's ropes right now, and LaFontaine is writhing, making a racket. We had no choice but to tie the poor thing, so off the rails, to the bedposts. The parasites seem to have lodged themselves into our friend's brain and now they're working overtime. I catch Carm providing a bit of comfort while she head-bangs to the sound of the techno-pop crap from the stage downstairs.

I prep for my daily update. Perry ordered me to stop vlogging, but I feel it's my obligation to keep everyone at Silas informed, so here we go. "It's finals week, which means junk food, caffeine and parties. But somewhere in an underground hideaway, a horrific sacrifice is being prepped. That's the bad news. Fear not, we do have good news as well. We found information on an evil-stopping sword that's going to level the playing field. The mother of all vamp-killing weapons. It's going to be a game changer. I know it."

"I can't believe LaFontaine lost J. P.," Carmilla grumbles. "Now we're down a resource."

"Misplaced," LaFontaine corrects her, still twisting and turning. The parasites are really having their way.

I turn to Carm. "You're going to head out soon to get the sword, yeah?"

"Soon."

I take her hand. "I'll feel so much better once you've got that. It'll mean we have a real chance against your mother. You know?" I rub my temples.

"Are you okay?" Carmilla asks tenderly.

"That necklace did a number on me. My whole head is pulsating." Carmilla comes over to massage my temples. "That feels a-mazing," I say. This is the most relaxed I've been since … I got here.

"You need to dial it back a notch, Hollis. I have to keep you and your friends safe. Hang here until I get back. Don't put yourself out there until we have a surefire plan."

"But I do have a plan," I say. "Remember all the people who watched the videos and wanted to help? We can call on them."

"Laura —" Carmilla cautions.

I interrupt. "No, listen. I bet they don't want to lose their friends to a vampire cult any more than we do. We could be the Silas Army."

"This is not a solid plan," she argues.

I'm not backing down. "We could fan out across the campus and search every basement until we find them. You get the sword. I'll rally the troops. It's a plan."

Carm tries to stop me but I bolt before she can. I know exactly what I'm doing.

•

I lead the charge with a group of students from my dorm. We descend on the party plaza and I jump on the stage, grabbing the microphone. I scream over the noise of the workers, "Silas students, attention, please! Our dean isn't who she pretends to be! She's an imposter! We think she kidnaps students and kills them! She's going to murder five more if we don't find her first! I need your help!"

I never expect that people won't believe me. But I hear boos from the crowd, then a tomato hits me in the middle of my forehead so hard that it doesn't even splat. My reinforcements get pelted and soon tomato innards coat the stage and some of the students. I wave to Danny, who's dancing with her Summer Society squad. She turns her back to me even though I clearly could use a hand. I shield myself with a trash can lid and dodge my way through the hostile crowd.

"Hey, Hollis!" I hear, turning to see a group of Zetas. I've never been happier to see them. They'll help me.

But they are despondent. "Dude, Kirsch and Will are gone," some guy in a baseball cap says. "Like, we can't find them and it's taco night. Kirsch never misses tacos. They're his favorite. Have you seen either of them?"

I have a bad feeling about this. "No."

"We were counting on you. You were our only hope."

Dejected, they continue their search. I get hit a few more times before a random paintball fight breaks out. I dodge that and find safety in my room.

"What the hell happened, Hollis?" Carmilla wipes the cuts on my arm with antiseptic, and it stings like hell. She gives me a bag of frozen peas for my forehead.

"When I jumped on the stage to tell everyone that the dean was a killer and planned to sacrifice five students, things got dicey. Some kids started launching tomatoes. I got hit in the head with one that wasn't ripe. I tried to get some help from Danny and her Summer Society sisters but she shunned me."

"I'll kick her ass," Carmilla says, all defensive.

"She can really hold a grudge. Anyway, the Zetas showed up. You know they love a good tomato toss, but they didn't even join in because they were looking for Kirsch. He and Will are missing. So much for my plan. And now the campus is a war zone."

Carmilla cups my cheek. "At least you're in one piece," she says. "I'll be back. I'm going to find that sword to put an end to this."

"Good luck."

I post a quick update when she leaves, then sign off for the day. But I'm so distracted that I accidentally click the last file with webcam footage of the past few days, and suddenly I see myself on screen, spewing words in a different voice that's familiar.

I turn up the volume. Carmilla is there.

The face is mine, the voice is not.

It's the dean's. "If you can keep your little pet here from making more trouble, I'll let you have her and take someone else instead," she says.

Carmilla steps into the frame. "How could I ever trust you?"

This is officially a freak show.

"How about a gesture of good faith?" Carmilla nods to me or her mother.

Oh my God. This crazy bitch took possession of my body and Carmilla didn't tell me? Why would she keep this from me? I thought she cared about me. How could I have been stupid enough to trust my heart to her?

I force myself to return to the footage. Possessed Me yells out to the hallway, "Will, why don't you bring in your friend?" I watch in horror as Kirsch bounces in, with Will following behind, sullen and surly as ever.

Kirsch greets Possessed Me. "Hey, Laura, Will said you needed help, and I was like, let's do this. Superman and the Zetas. Superheroes. We're all in."

I fast-forward and catch Carmilla snarling at Possessed Me, "I thought your hungry Nite-Light only wanted virgins?"

"I see you've been reading Barclay's transcriptions. That man was obsessed. It's hardly that romantic. We take girls because the world's going to grind them up anyway, so we're actually doing them a favor. Simple." Seeing my mouth move but hearing the dean's voice is chilling.

I have to stop watching. It's just too painful. I chose Carmilla over Danny. I fell for her bullshit like all the girls before me. And she kept this from me? How could I be so naive? The war outside is raging on. So is the war inside me. My door opens. If it's Carmilla, I may kill her myself.

But it's Perry. She has her arm around LaFontaine, who's moaning, "I just want to go to the party. It sounds like so much fun."

Perry rubs her friend's back. "Let's get you some tea or water."

"I want the Fuzzy Dagons that are at the party, please," LaFontaine begs.

Perry looks to me for help. "Hey, LaFontaine, there's no

party," I pipe up. "I was just there. It's like a battle for the Silas courtyard out there. That isn't the sound of anyone having fun. Trust me, I was caught in the crossfire of the paintball exchange."

LaFontaine, in a funk, sits on the bed. Perry mouths, "Thanks," then tries to help with a drink of water. She's been hell-bent on flushing all the "bad stuff" out of LaFontaine's system since her friend came back to us.

For the next ten minutes, Perry and LaFontaine watch the video. "So how did the dean possess you?" Perry asks.

"No idea." It must have happened after I put on that necklace?

"I knew that vampire was bad news. If she tries anything" — Perry pulls two stakes from her backpack — "I'll stake her. She isn't getting near Sus — LaFontaine."

LaFontaine leans in to Perry. "Thank you. I've noticed. I know this is difficult for you."

Perry hugs her friend. "It's not hard. It's still you."

LaFontaine returns to the screen, staring at it in disbelief. "They're going to kill Kirsch instead of you? The dean kidnapped me? You were the dean?"

"It's okay. Things are a little fuzzy. We'll take care of everything," Perry says reassuringly.

I glance in her direction. "You were on point about this place. Silas is a nightmare. There is no Dr. Seuss happening here. It's more like *American Horror Story* than *The Grinch*. And *The Grinch* was pretty damn bad."

Then Carmilla comes rushing in, out of breath and without a sword. When she sees the video cued up, she knows she's busted. Perry jumps up off the bed, stake in hand. "Don't take another step, bloodsucker."

Carmilla moves past Perry. "What is this?"

"Don't act like you don't know," I bark, then hit Play. Suddenly I come to life as the dean. "What's it going to be? I can take out the king of Fraternity Row or your little girl toy. Your choice." Kirsch cowers next to Possessed Me.

Carmilla and her mother, I mean me, are nose to nose.

"It's simple, Carmilla. Laura is safe if she stops interfering in my business. But if she gets in the way again, she's history. I'll take him and you two can go on your merry way. Do we have a deal?"

Carmilla watches herself on video. "It's a deal, Mother."

There's stone-cold silence in the room.

I can barely look at her. "Were you even going to mention any of this to me? You know, how your mother somehow became me and used me to hurt my friends? Were you even going to get the sword?"

She reaches for me. "Laura, please give me a chance to —"

"Oh, hell no. That might work on the laundry list of girls you've slept with at Silas but not on me."

"She promised to leave us alone," she starts to explain.

I put my finger in her face. "Sure, *if* you let her kill my friends."

"She swore she'd back off and that you'd always be safe. I didn't have a choice."

"Please," she begs, her voice cracking.

"And you so had a choice."

Choking back tears, she tries to get close. "My choice was you. I chose you."

I throw my hands up in front of her. I can't do this. "Just leave. You broke my feelings. We're done here."

I watch her slink away, praying I don't burst into tears. This vampire not only took my blood, she stole my heart.

· EIGHTEEN ·

The two sides of my brain have been fighting each other since Carmilla left. One side feels battered and defeated, like it will never fall for someone again. The other side is pumping its fist in the air and celebrating that I dodged a bullet. Confession: my stomach is with the first half of my brain.

It doesn't help that LaFontaine has spent the better part of the day twirling in circles, playing air guitar and singing "Girls Just Want to Have Fun" at top volume. Perry and I eye-speak, then tackle and restrain her friend once more. The parasites have really kicked it up a notch. "We have to get to the party, we just have to," LaFontaine whimpers, squirming like a snake.

"There is no party, LaFontaine. I wish there was, I would take you," Perry says.

I let the two of them hash it out while I get back to my vlog.

I look directly into the camera and begin a new post. "So. College isn't turning out like I thought it would. If you've been following, you know that a few weeks ago the dean — who is beyond unscru- pulous — kidnapped my roommate Betty to feed some brain- devouring hungry light under the earth as part of her intricate plan to sacrifice five students. I know, it's a lot to absorb."

LaFontaine's screams take over. "I promise there's a party! I need to go! Perry, if you care about me ... the party!"

I power on. "Sorry about the outburst. Back to the dean. I thought I could rescue Betty, but instead all I've managed to do is get my friends brain-sucked and my heart broken. Side note, I'm pretty sure I've flunked out of freshman year. I'm at a crossroads. If I do nothing, I can just go home but then I'd have to accept that I can't make a difference. That my actions won't save the world." I pause. "I can't do that."

LaFontaine bursts out again. "The party! I have to go! We're missing it! It's starting without us!"

Perry wraps her friend in a hug. "Calm down. There. Is. No. Party."

LaFontaine is insistent. "There is and it's now! The light is over the party! Follow it and you'll see all the people."

Perry rubs LaFontaine's back, trying to help.

Holy shit, I get it! The light is the hungry light. The celebra- tion before the sacrifice that was in the Sumerian book. "That's the party."

"Not helping, Hollis," Perry says, trying to shut me down.

"No, no. I know what LaFontaine is talking about. When Carmilla read the translation from the big book, it said their world 'narrows to celebration.' What if it was supposed to be 'narrows to *the* celebration'? LaFontaine, is there a bright light at the party?"

"Yes. A glittering, bright party light."

I kneel in front of LaFontaine. "Do you know how to get to the party?"

Perry is spitting nails, which I get. She loves her friend and doesn't want to put anyone in harm's way, but I've come this far. I can't just back down. I try to soften my approach. Not be so obvious.

"Yes! Untie me before we miss it."

Perry jumps up. "Stop this right now. No one is going anywhere. It's too dangerous. We'll all get killed."

LaFontaine hesitates.

"LaFontaine, if you don't want to," I say, "I won't make you. I don't even think we have a real shot against the dean and her followers, the Vamp Army. But you never know ..." I'm not even trying to be convincing. I have to get to that party. I have to try to save everyone.

Perry is not on board. "I have a post-finals brunch to plan and I don't like you hassling my friend into doing this. There are things more important than winning."

I bite back. "True, but sometimes you have to fight anyway."

She digests that, nods and we untie LaFontaine, who, once

freed, drifts to the door. Before I follow, I turn back to the camera.

"Carmilla ... oh, never mind, you know."

Perry and I follow LaFontaine with blind faith toward the Lustig Theater Building. "Yes, the theater. This is where they brought me. I remember all the trees and the name on the building."

The entry is dark and spooky, and that's before we're led down a spiral staircase covered in a curtain of cobwebs. There's a maze of caves down here, dark and dank. "This is creep on crack," I quip.

Finally, I hear some muffled sounds. Perry and I duck behind LaFontaine when we hear shrill voices, and soon we land at the lip of an enormous cavern. "Holy hell, they're all here. They're really here," LaFontaine whispers back to us. "I did good."

I peek over LaFontaine's shoulder and see the dean, her vampire army, Kirsch and the girls with their backs to us. Even Betty is here, glued to Natalie.

"Yeah, you did. Now we need a plan," I suggest.

Will is stalking around the group like a tarantula. Prepping for the sacrifice, no doubt.

"I told you there was a party." LaFontaine is hell-bent on jamming this down Perry's throat.

"Okay, okay," Perry replies, "you were right. But it's not quite the party you're expecting. Instead of dancing there will be killing."

"Killing?" LaFontaine gasps.

"They're going to sacrifice our friends. Unless we can stop them," I say.

"How are we going to do that?" LaFontaine asks.

"I'm thinking," I respond.

"Let's rush them," Perry proposes. "Take them off guard. Take out Will and the dean first. On my go. *Go!*"

Holy shit, it's on.

As soon as she hears us, the dean draws a knife from her boot and charges our friends, holding them at bay. Really wish I could summon up Harry and his Expelliarmus spell. Her minions scatter, trying to surround us.

Will swirls and meets the tip of Perry's stake, which she drives into his heart. Blood splatters everywhere.

Kirsch gasps. "Sorry, sweetie," Perry apologizes mid-fray.

He shrugs. "It's cool. Bro dude had it coming."

I snag a gargoyle and clock one of the vamps. We have to rid ourselves of them to get away with our friends. I keep swinging until a lasso lands around my waist. I can't keep my feet on the ground as I'm being dragged down a path. Perry jumps out in front of me. "I'll save you!" I hear Perry yell, right before another vampire puts her in a headlock.

Our plan is falling apart.

"Nooooooo." That's LaFontaine's unmistakable voice. A group of rogue vampires from Team Dean pin down Kirsch and subdue the others. They must have been hiding in one of the side caverns.

That's the last thing I see before Perry and I get tossed into a dark broom closet with a steel door. Where is a sonic screwdriver when you need one?

"Shit, we're going to be dinner."

Perry gulps. "Crap. We were so close."

I reach in my back pocket. "They forgot to take my phone, yes. Vampires aren't the sharpest."

"Text Danny — she'll know what to do," Perry suggests.

Oh God, Danny. "Not sure she would even reply to me, let alone help me at this point."

"She will. It's who she is."

That stings.

"Do you even get a signal down here?" Perry asks.

The phone has no bars. "Not in this spot."

I test every corner of the closet, holding the phone as high and low as possible in search of a signal. Huzzah! One lone, gorgeous, glowing bar that can save our lives.

Trapped in basement of Dudley chapel under Lustig Theater Building. Dean has us. Come quick. Bring weapons.

I check it over and over, shaking the phone like that will help. It takes forever but the text goes through.

"*Yes!* Now, we wait."

"We're going to be okay, aren't we, Laura?"

Now is not the time to bring up my doubts. Fear is creeping in — I can see it on Perry's face. "Yeah, we're going to be fine. Once we're back at the dorm, we'll laugh about all of this."

No, we won't.

"I'll bake brownies."

Okay, then.

Still and quiet turn into thunderous noise. A battering ram bashes down the door. Danny and a cavalry of Summer Society sisters and Zetas greet us, armed with tridents and the traditional salted herring.

We join them and charge the vampire lines. Perhaps not the smartest but we have numbers and energy. Lots of adrenaline is flowing.

The Zetas use the tridents to ward off the first line of vamps, who all crumble to the ground. Those weapons leave gnarly wounds.

Danny's squad attacks two vamps with flat irons and broomsticks, both surprisingly effective weapons. I'm wielding a mop that packs a mean punch when swung like a baseball bat.

"Behind you, Hollis!" I hear Perry yell. I whip around just as a vampire is about to bite my neck. I drop him with my killer mop.

Two of the Zetas start hurling the herring at the vamps. Those suckers sting when they hit you in the face. I hear the vampires yelp as they drop to the ground. Danny finishes them off with a flat iron to the temple.

Good thing Perry whittled all those stakes — she's firing them off like a pro. Kirsch's karate is coming in handy as he takes on anyone in his path with kicks and chops.

Sticking together, we've got them backed up against a wall.

Then there's a rumbling so loud that I can't hear myself think. I plug my ears with my fingers.

"Oh my God, check this out!" Danny shouts. An incandescent light emanating from the bottom of the pit shines bright and starts to rise.

"It's like the sun is coming up underground, it's so bright," I remark. An earsplitting hum of thousands of voices beckons us to walk toward them. We are all so attracted to the light that it takes us over, and like zombies we start walking right for the edge. I mean, we are heading for the pit. The drop has to be over two thousand feet. Jagged rocks all around it.

When I'm about two feet from the edge, a giant pantherlike cat grabs me by the neck and yanks me back like a rag doll. Shocked, I watch it shrink, then shift.

It's Carmilla. Brandishing a sword. *The* sword. As she swings it, we watch it swallow the light bit by bit with each stroke. I tear up and reach for her.

The dean screeches from behind, "I will destroy all of you!" Before I can inch out of the way, she shifts into a swarm of shadows like crows, scratching and clawing at us. The piercing cries are deafening.

"Carmilla!" I plead.

Perry and Danny swing brooms at the dean, taking a few swipes of her claws that draw blood. But she's fast and skilled. A vamp clips Kirsch with a bat, breaking his arm. Kirsch squeals. That had to hurt.

I see Betty and the other girls emerge from the wings of a cavern. They jump into the fray, swinging their fists wildly like warriors until the dean shifts back into a woman again. She comes right at me. As she's about to turn me into roadkill, Carmilla hollers and throws herself between us. "Run, Hollis!"

Her mother slices at her, narrowly missing. I run as instructed, turning to see Carmilla deck her mother with the sword hilt and tumble into the pit.

It's too late. The light is everywhere. People are climbing into the lip of the chasm, trying to fling themselves in. So many figures in the light. I see a girl. She looks like the girl from my dream. She reaches for Carmilla. It must be Ell.

In that split second, Carm turns back to me. "You know, I really hate this heroic vampire bullshit." I watch her leap down, driving the sword right into the heart of the light. The light snaps and twitches like it's alive. All the ghosts throw back their heads, screaming, before tumbling into the darkness together.

I kneel down near the spot where I just watched Carmilla die while the waterworks pour down my face. My shirt is soaked.

It was an epic battle to the death.

"It was always you. My hero," I whisper into vast nothingness.

•

I stumble back to the dorm with my crew after the battle, blood-soaked clothes and all. I take out our first-aid kit and start getting cleaned up. The peroxide stings like hell. I pass out bandages.

Kirsch, pouting, has his arm in a sling. "Why did she have to break my Frisbee arm? Women are so mean."

I pat his good arm. "You'll be fine soon. At least you can still pick up a taco with your left hand." That makes him happy.

Danny and Perry are bedraggled and covered in red as well. I pass them some towels and antiseptic wipes. LaFontaine dotes on Perry, nursing her wounds.

Betty sits on the edge of her bed wrapped in an emergency blanket. "I can't wait to transfer to Princeton. I bet this doesn't happen there."

"This doesn't happen anywhere but here," LaFontaine states with some authority. "I can't believe we won."

I burst into tears. "But Carmilla died."

· NINETEEN ·

We're all traumatized but I'm fairly certain that I'm the only one missing every single thing about my vampire ex-girlfriend who died saving all of us from her vindictive mother. I try to choke back the tears but the sobs keep coming. Danny rubs my back.

"Let's get you tucked in." She guides me to my bed. She's given up on hating me. War does that to you.

Danny takes my place at command central to update the Silas students. All I can do is watch and listen from my bed in the fetal position. Perry joins her, back to her starched self.

"Hi, students. Laura wanted us to update you about the big win we had yesterday. She's a bit under the weather, recovering from the battle," Danny opens.

Perry continues, "Here's how it went down. LaFontaine led us to the Lustig Theater Building, where the dean and her vampire army were holed up with the missing Silas students, preparing to feed them to the light. We tracked them through a maze below the building."

LaFontaine chimes in. "I still can't believe you used me as a human homing beacon."

"Desperate times," Perry says.

LaFontaine corrects her. "Oh no. That was badass hard core. We do not apologize for that. Ever."

Perry turns to hug LaFontaine. "I missed you, weirdo."

"Control freak."

Back together looks really good on them. Danny coughs. "And …"

Perry continues her explanation after veering off track momentarily. "I'll spare you the misstep when we got caught up in the broom closet. It happens. Once the Summer Society and the Zetas busted us out, the confrontation began. They were all there — the dean, the vampires, Kirsch and the other victims — at the lip of this enormous chasm filled with a glistening light."

I see LaFontaine shudder. Perry throws her arm around her friend, whose head drops on her shoulder.

I get up and go over to the camera. "All of the humans started walking right for the edge because what could you do but give yourself to the light? In a split second, I was yanked backward by a pantherlike animal. When I was a safe distance away, the beast shrank and shifted, and there stood Carmilla. With a sword. The only thing that could destroy the light and save us all." Sadness creeps in once more. "And she leapt forward, driving the sword right into the heart of the light. We watched it flicker, then die out, taking all the vampire ghosts and darkness with it. It cost Carmilla her life. She wasn't guilty of what we accused her of. We were all wrong. I was wrong." Danny puts her arm around me.

LaFontaine moves into focus to finish the story while the nonstop tears flow down my cheeks. "Once the light was extinguished, I guess the brain parasites died. That's when everyone woke up more or less."

"I was at a wine and cheese," Natalie says. "That's it. Holding a glass of rosé."

"I was on a campus tour. I didn't even want to go to Silas!" Betty yells. Perry moves the webcam on her. "But we were still trapped in a cavern in complete darkness with a crapload of flesh-eating vampires. Okay, it wasn't totally black since the walls had glowing puffballs on the them, thanks to the Alchemy Club. Turns out they're good for something."

I crawl back into bed.

"It was like having a bar fight in black light," Kirsch adds. "Totally rad, until a vampire broke my arm. That's when Summer Psycho saved my bacon."

"That part was accidental," Danny notes.

Kirsch pulls her close. "Even so, when you save a Zeta's life, you become an honorary Zeta. For life. We're legit a family. You even get a cool trident." He's so proud it's endearing.

Danny plants her forehead in the palm of her hand. "All the vampires surrendered. Carmilla's mom, the dean, did not."

"She was clinging with her claws to the cliff face about fifty feet down," Perry says with a laugh.

Danny chuckles. "Yeah, she was screaming at us that she would be back and we would all pay for what we'd done."

Kirsch gets his puppy on, jumping around. "That's when hottie Hollis pushed a rock that was hanging out on the edge. *Bam*, right on the dean, squashing her like a bug."

LaFontaine peps up. "Even better than that? Now that the evil dean is gone, the new administration is going to have to heed my long list of health and safety concerns. I win!"

Perry touches LaFontaine's arm and gestures toward me. I don't miss that. "Sorry, Laura," she says.

I say words that aren't true in response. "It's okay."

Perry tries to comfort me. "You did it. You saved Betty. You saved almost everybody."

"Almost" rings loudly in my ears and heart.

I roll over, curl up and cry an ocean of tears.

· TWENTY ·

The last few days have been a blur. I've just been replaying Carmilla's last words to me over and over on a loop. When I close my eyes, I see her fall into the abyss to her death, her mother's threats still reverberating. All to save me.

I finally force myself to take a shower, but even the shower makes me think of Carmilla. Her hair is still in the drain. I really miss her. I haven't had a single cookie since she died. I mean, I'm happy Betty is back but I miss all of Carmilla's crazy. I refuse to throw out the last container of "soy milk" no matter how many times Perry tells me I need to do it.

What I need is for Carmilla to be here. With me.

Betty is slowly but surely packing up Carmilla's things to make room for her own stuff once more. It feels so final. Even though Betty wants to go to Princeton, she's hanging here until the transfer comes through.

Betty cleans up her bed, tossing Carmilla's belongings into one small box. She heads into the bathroom with her cleaning supplies. Between Betty and Perry, they could open up a maid service.

"I need all the bleach. Carmilla was a pig." I'm trying not to go off on her but Betty is being slightly inconsiderate. I mean, granted she has no idea what Carm means … meant to me, but she did play a huge part in saving her, so maybe she could ease up on the harsh commentary.

"She rescued your ass, so show some respect. It's only hair."

LaFontaine peeks in. "Do you want to grab some breakfast?" They've been super attentive since everything with Carm went down. Everyone has. Even though her feelings were hurt, Danny let me slide with a passing grade and she's been making excuses to check up on me ever since.

"I'm not really hungry."

"You have to eat, even if it's just toast," LaFontaine reminds me sweetly, sauntering by Betty, who's muttering to her cereal. Betty grabs the milk and freaks out when she sees the blood in the soy milk container.

"Blood? Why is there blood in the milk container? I have to get out of here." She hightails it out the door before I can explain.

A rumble comes from outside.

"I'm starting to get used to the aftershocks," LaFontaine says. "Is that bad?"

"So I can't help noticing that you and J. P. have been attached at the hip in the library since the upheaval. I was glad he turned up."

LaFontaine cringes. "Perry is having a tough time with that. And I know you're having a hard time with Carmilla being gone, regardless of her past."

My eyes mist over. "I know she was a terrible roommate and did some pretty awful things, and that one big gesture doesn't erase all that she did. But she was my terrible roommate, and she made the stupid gesture for me. No, it wasn't stupid, it was romantic."

I can't stop the sobbing. LaFontaine hands me some tissues. A knock at the door forces me to catch my breath. We finally got everyone to agree to knock before barging in. Well, kind of. Perry flings the door open all agitated.

"Hollis. I have news. Sit down, I can't have you lose it on me. It's big."

"Oh God. I can't handle any more," I blurt out, wiping away my tears.

She throws both hands up. "Listen to me. Kirsch and his Zeta bros were throwing cherry bombs into the pit under the Lustig."

"More fireworks? I care less than less." I'm dog-tired of all of this.

"They stumbled on something you might be interested in."

I doubt it, but I feign interest in the spirit of being a decent friend. Before she can finish her story, Danny bursts in carrying Carmilla. She's battered and covered in dust. Shocked doesn't begin to cover how I feel.

I rush to her side. "Are you alive?"

She doesn't answer. Her head flops onto Danny's shoulder.

Danny responds, catching her breath. "We found her in the pit. She wasn't moving, but I think she's breathing. Vampires don't really die, do they?" Danny asks.

She's translucent. "She needs blood!" I scream, grabbing the container from the fridge. I tip it to her lips. "Please be alive, you goofy vampire. Don't be dead. I have so much more to tell you. We have so much more to do."

Carmilla drains the entire container and starts to pink up. I see her chest heave. She's breathing. "Well, that was a kick," she chokes out. I wrap her in a bear hug and squeeze her, not wanting to ever let go. Perry clears her throat. Crap, I forgot my room was packed with people.

Again.

I shy away. "Hey."

She props herself on her elbow. "Hey, yourself."

Danny clears her throat. "I'm gonna head out." A symphony of "me, toos" joins in. I want to scream "Thank God" but I refrain, turning my attention to Carmilla once the door closes.

"Are you hurt? I didn't mean to hug you so hard."

She smirks. "Oh, I liked that part."

"I thought you were dead. We all did and now that you're not, I'm so happy. I mean, I know you're going through a lot with your mother and your girlfriend."

She slips her arm around my waist, guiding me toward her, barely touching her lips to mine. She moves back ever so slightly and looks into my eyes. "She's not my girlfriend. That was literally a lifetime ago. You are mine now."

Melting.

She takes my bottom lip between her teeth very lightly, then kisses me in what might be the sweetest, longest kiss of my life. I come up momentarily for air. "I know you didn't do that just for me but it was so badass." She kisses me again. And again.

"Of course I did it for you, cupcake."

· TWENTY-ONE ·

Kissing makes you work up an appetite.

"This is the first time since the battle that I've seen you eat anything other than the blood you chug," I tease Carm. She bares her teeth at me, chomping down on a slice of extra-cheese pizza.

"You might have heard that vampires like to sink their teeth into just about anything."

I point at my neck where she left her mark. "I have." Finishing my fourth slice, I get up to turn the webcam on.

Carm tugs on the tail of my shirt. "Seriously, today? I can't have one day without that thing?"

"You don't want to record this for posterity?"

"Posterity has a way of biting you in the ass. Pardon the pun. Not really." She plants a light kiss on my cheek, massages my shoulders. I feel her breath on my neck.

"Don't even think about it."

Carmilla laughs.

"Come sit next to me."

She pulls up a chair.

I chide her. "You know everyone wants to know how you survived." I move closer, get some sexy in my voice. "I'll make it worth your while."

She rolls her eyes but agrees. "It turns out —"

Before she can even start her tale, LaFontaine bursts in, in full-blown panic mode. So much for the new rule of knocking. Perry trails them.

"I seriously hate this place," Carmilla says.

"Where is it? I need the book. Now. The big Sumerian book? Where. Is. It? Why is no one paying attention to me?" Zero to one-eighty is LaFontaine's specialty.

"I think Betty was using it as a tray to eat dinner in bed last night. Check under the covers."

LaFontaine throws back the sheets and snatches it up, riffling through the pages. "Ugh, I can't read Sumerian. Help me, vampire queen."

I implore Carm with my eyes. She takes the book from LaFontaine, who is borderline hysterical. "Where's the part about the Lophilformes? Where is that page? We need that page."

"Slow down," Carmilla says.

"Tell me to do whatever you want, just find the page." LaFontaine paces back and forth.

"LaFontaine, what's going on?" I ask. "Take a breath."

"J. P. and I were in the library researching the aftershocks. I was confused about the light. Like why would something that feeds on mental energy force people to throw themselves into the pit of death. J. P. agrees. It doesn't make sense." Then, after a dramatic pause, "Unless ..."

Carm groans loudly.

"... there's something else down there."

Just no.

Silence envelops the room. Carm has her finger on the edge of the page about this light. She hesitantly holds it out to LaFontaine. Slowly, excruciatingly painfully ... LaFontaine reaches down and flips the page.

Carmilla groans. "This only says something about the light being the lure. And underneath it ..."

I fixate on the picture. "Oh God. Look at the mouth. It's like a wide-mouth fish with razor-sharp teeth."

Rumbling in the distance interrupts us. We stare at one another before Carm breaks the quiet. Realizing the ugly truth, Carm shares what no one wants to hear: "We didn't kill it."

I speak up, "Bright side, we stopped the sacrifice."

Carmilla says, "Dark side, the sacrifice should have appeased it. That didn't happen, so now the light is mad. Am I close?"

Perry cries out, "Why can't anything be normal?"

"Because Silas," I say.

"Truth," LaFontaine says.

"Now what are we gonna do?" I ask.

"All I want to do is be in the library with J. P."

"You know he's a hologram, right?" Carm asks.

"Don't judge him," LaFontaine wails.

"Can we focus on the bigger picture right now?" I ask, mania setting in.

LaFontaine gets serious. "It's obvious. Back to war we go. Defeat the evil. Take back our campus once more. I'll get J. P."

Perry keeps shaking her head. "No. No. No. A thousand times *no!*"

I yell, "Bring it on!"

Carm just shakes her head. "Here we go again. Why can't we just have a nice vampire–normal girl relationship?"